MOUSE IN THE HOUSE

A MAGICAL MOUSE CAPER

DEANNA DRAKE

Fine Skylark Media, P.O. Box 1505

Lake Forest, California 92609-1505

Mouse in the House: A Magical Mouse Caper

ISBN: 978-1-957691-01-5

www.DeAnnaDrake.com

DeAnna@DeAnnaDrake.com

Cover designed by Sleepy Fox Studio.

Interior illustrations created in Midjourney by Merrie Destefano. Interior design also by Merrie Destefano.

CONTENTS

To Skye, the newest critter in our family

MOUSE IN THE HOUSE

BY DEANNA DRAKE

This house mouse might be a walking, talking wonder, but it'll take every one of his special gifts to catch his landlady's killer.

A freak accident at birth gave house mouse Max the ability to speak, but an ego-bruising life lesson taught him to keep his muzzle shut. Now, he leads a quiet life at the Reginald Arms, a struggling boardinghouse with a troubled past.

At least he did until cupcake-making marvel Darla Jo Masters moves in to help her aunt run the place and lures him from the shadows with the delicious scent of her freshly baked treats. She's also whip-

ping up ideas for home improvements to keep her aunt out of bankruptcy.

The only problem is, Landlady Jenkins doesn't want Darla Jo's help, and she might be trying to sabotage them by working with the local newspaper to sensationalize an old family scandal and rumors of a resident ghost.

When Landlady Jenkins turns up dead, Darla Jo is the prime suspect. The cops think it's an open-and-shut case, but Max is standing by his friend. Can this timid little critter save an innocent girl, or will his vow of silence allow a killer to get away with murder?

If you're a reader who likes cozy mysteries, cute critters, and cupcakes, *Mouse in the House* is for you.

ONE

It had to be the cupcakes. Darla Jo had shooed me off to my hiding spot under the staircase while she spent the afternoon refining a secret recipe, but I knew what the kitchen looked like when she baked. All those batter-crusted mixing bowls, frosting-covered spoons, and pans filled with crumbly goodness were the stuff of dreams, but Landlady Jenkins didn't see it that way. She had little patience for her niece's messes, and she wasn't shy about making it known.

That had to be what all the yelling was about. If I was a braver mouse, I would have rushed to Darla Jo's defense, but I wasn't brave. Not anymore.

Besides, the last time Landlady Jenkins spotted me, she'd grabbed a broom and chased me up the stairs. I'd gotten away, of course, but she'd slipped on a step and ended up in the hospital for three days.

That's why she walks with a cane now, and I bet the sight of me would rile her up all over again. There's no telling what might happen if she spotted me poking around.

I can't say I entirely regret the accident, though. It was during that hospital stay that Darla Jo Masters showed up with her bluebell eyes and vanilla-scented hair, which hangs in soft, brown waves over her shoulders. She told Landlady Jenkins she'd come to help run the boardinghouse so her aunt could rest and recuperate.

At least, that's how it started.

Once Darla Jo saw all the past-due notices in the mail, she decided her aunt needed more than a few pillows and afternoons off her feet.

She's made it her mission to set the place straight, and every week, she comes up with new ideas to make it profitable. Her latest is a doozy too.

"The Reginald Arms has been in our family for six generations," I heard her tell her aunt over breakfast. "We can't let a bank take it. There's so much potential here with the beach only a few blocks away. The tourist hotels sell out during the summer. I'm sure we could attract some of that business if we tried. We also have something those hotels don't. We have history. My dad loved to tell me stories about how this used to be one of the grandest houses in the city. We should be using that to our advantage."

Landlady Jenkins wrinkled her nose like she always did. "What advantage? We're a boarding-house. Nothing more, nothing less."

But the place isn't much of a boardinghouse, either. There are five en suite rooms carved into the upstairs floor, and only one paying tenant since a rainstorm flooded out the other two three months ago.

Still, I wasn't entirely sold on Darla Jo's latest suggestion. It was like she had never taken a good look at the place, because if she had, she'd see dirt where grass should be, bare wood where paint should be, and a porch step that was broken long before I moved in a year ago.

It was a wretched sight, even on a good day.

What self-respecting tourist would choose to stay in a dump like this?

For me, however, it was perfect. The building was a mess, but so was I the first time I saw it. I was looking for a place to hide away and hide out, and this place fit the bill. I sneaked inside, found a cozy spot under the stairs, and it's been home ever since.

I got so used to the miserable conditions, I stopped noticing them until Darla Jo showed up. Then, somehow, without even trying, that girl made everything better. Sometimes I wonder why she puts up with this place, considering the way Landlady Jenkins treats her.

Lucky for me, Darla Jo tolerates it. And even luckier for me, when it gets really bad, she bakes. After their last fight, she made snickerdoodle cupcakes and raspberry white chocolate cupcakes on the same day.

So, when she told me she wanted to be alone to tinker with a new recipe, I suspected something was troubling her. At first, the yelling didn't even surprise me.

Another day, another argument. That was practically their daily routine.

Except something was different this time. Landlady Jenkins wasn't yelling at Darla Jo. It was the other way around.

I pressed my ear to the widest crack in the wood and tried to listen in. It was the first time I'd heard Darla Jo yell. Ever. She hadn't even raised her voice the afternoon she caught me taste-testing one of her double chocolate cupcakes that first time. They were so heavenly, so absolutely scrumptious, I'd completely forgotten to use my mouse sounds.

I'd tried to resist those sweet treats, but I hadn't smelled anything that good in months. Maybe not in my whole life. Then, once I tasted that decadent goodness, I couldn't stop myself.

When she'd spotted me, she didn't scream. She didn't jump up on a chair. She didn't do any of the things humans usually do when they see me or one of my kind. She just said, rather calmly, "Excuse me."

Too startled to think straight, I'd spun around with my arms in the air and begged forgiveness. Actually, my exact words were, "I'm so sorry! I didn't mean to eat the whole thing."

When I realized I was speaking in my natural voice, the one I've had since birth and which I've solemnly sworn never to use again, I clamped my mouth shut and made a mad dash for the closest hole in the wall.

It didn't occur to me that she wasn't screaming or running or chasing me with a broom until I heard her say, still calmly, "So, you like my cupcakes? If you come back, you can have another one."

I figured it was a trick, but there was something

about her—something as sweet as the little cake I'd been nibbling—that made me trust her.

So, I went back, and when I saw that smile on her lips and in her eyes, I introduced myself. "Hello. I'm Maxwell Mouse, formerly of the Arabella Beach Pier Mouses and presently sole mouse resident of the Reginald Arms."

Was it reckless? I guess it was. But if you've ever had one of Darla Jo's exceptional treats, you know they're worth any risk. And even that first day, I somehow knew Darla Jo was exceptional too. When she smiled, dimples kissed both cheeks and her dark chocolate eyes disappeared behind happy crescents. A girl like that wouldn't hurt a fly, I told myself, let alone a mouse.

Yet that angry voice in the other room definitely belonged to Darla Jo, even if I couldn't make out every word.

"How...?"

"Why...?"

"What possessed you?"

What had the old woman done to upset Darla Jo so much?

When my whiskers twitched, a sign that trouble was near, I knew I had to do something. I shimmied through the crack in the wood panel and raced through the empty dining room to the kitchen.

As I neared, I could hear Darla Jo more clearly.

"Why would you say those things to a reporter?"

"I didn't say anything to a reporter, not that it's any of your business," Landlady Jenkins shot back. "I don't have to explain myself to you."

I hurried across the floor until I reached the open door to the kitchen. From the narrow space beneath the door hinge, I could see my friend standing beside three racks of cupcakes cooling on the counter, a newspaper clenched in her fist.

Landlady Jenkins stood in front of the refrigerator, scowling at her, her fingers wrapped in a death grip around her cane. "If you actually read that trash, you'd know the story didn't come from me. That writer quotes somebody at the historical society, not me."

Darla Jo scanned the page. "Why would they go to the historical society? Did you tell them to do that? Did you tip them off?"

Landlady Jenkins busied herself wiping crumbs from the counter. It was a pointless effort considering the monumental mess in front of her. "I did no such thing. Maybe they followed me. How am I supposed to know?"

"Followed you? You went there? Why?"

"That's none of your business."

Darla Jo fumed. "Really? You've made it clear you hate my idea of turning this place into a bed and breakfast. Telling the world Carson Reginald was murdered here and that his ghost roams the halls is a great way to make sure that never happens. Awfully convenient, wouldn't you say? No one in their right mind would want to stay here now." She shook the newspaper at her aunt to emphasize her point.

"You have no idea what you're talking about. I've been operating this boardinghouse longer than you've been alive, and I watched my father run it before that, and his father before that. I don't need a college student telling me how to do my business."

"Graduate," Darla Jo mumbled. "I'm a college graduate."

"That's what you say, but I don't see a degree. Where's the degree?"

"It's in the mail. I spoke to somebody at the college, and they said there was a mix up with some of the names. It's on its way."

"Fine, so you get a degree, and you think you can take The Reginald away from me?"

Darla Jo closed her eyes and shook her head. "No one wants to take this place away from you, except your bank, and reminding the world that your grandfather's grandfather was murdered here by his own son and spreading some silly story that his ghost haunts the place isn't going to help you attract new tenants or tourists or anybody."

"They got that part wrong," Landlady Jenkins sneered back. "It's not Carson's ghost. It's his son, Alexander. The story my father told me was the young man was drunk and flew into a rage one night when his father refused to give him money to pay off a gambling debt. They fought. Alexander said his father had plenty of gold, and he practically tore the place apart looking for the stash. When Carson tried to stop him, that's when he fell down the stairs. He wasn't pushed, despite what people believed. When he sobered up, Alexander was filled with remorse, and his soul never found peace. That's why he haunts the corridors. I was going to call those newspaper people to tell them that. If they're going to print this drivel, they can at least get their facts straight."

"Is that really the point?" Darla Jo threw the newspaper on the counter, where it skidded between two dirty mixing bowls. "But, yes, please, ask them to print a correction. Let's keep our family's old dirty laundry in the public eye for another news cycle so no one will ever want to step foot in this place again."

Someone pounded on the kitchen door. Landlady Jenkins glanced at the clock and scowled before hobbling over to answer it. When she turned around to grab the knob, the edge of her cane caught the side of a chair and pulled her off balance.

The old woman tipped and swayed and was about to tumble, but Darla Jo caught her in time. As the woman's arms flailed, trying to regain her balance, her hand swiped across Darla Jo's cheek, leaving a sliver of red.

"Are you all right?" Darla Jo grabbed the cane and handed it back to her aunt, then rubbed her cheek.

"Good grief, who put that chair in the way? I'm fine. Don't make such a fuss." She planted the cane firmly, pulled open the door, and turned back without even looking at the delivery guy. "You're late. Again. I want my discount."

The pizza guy, a lanky young man in black-rimmed glasses, a red and white striped polo shirt with a Pepperoni Joe's logo on the chest, and a matching ball cap pulled low over his eyes, set the pizza box on the table beside the door. The smell of spicy meat, cheese, and tomato sauce filled the room.

"I keep telling you, Ms. Jenkins, your clock must be fast. The order slip says you called in at seven-oh-nine. It's only seven-twenty-five. The shop guarantees thirty minutes or sooner. Remember, I told you that yesterday."

And the day before that and the day before that. You'd think a woman who ordered pizza every night of the week would know the rules by now. But the delivery guy and I both knew her memory was just fine.

Complaining about the pizza being late even when it wasn't—and it never was—had become as much a daily ritual for Landlady Jenkins as complaining about Darla Jo's business suggestions.

The second part of this particular ritual was still playing out as she fished a single bill from her wallet and fiddled with her glasses as she examined it. Finally, she placed the bill in the young man's hand. "There now. You can keep the change."

He forced a smile. "Thank you, ma'am. With tips like this, I'll be able to afford graduate school any day now."

She scooped up the box and took it to the last clear space on the counter. "Good for you. You could teach my grandniece here a thing or two about the value of a dollar."

The delivery guy must have sensed she was trying to lure him into something, so he waved at Darla Jo and made a hasty exit.

"You know that was only a dollar, right? That pizza cost almost twenty. You should have given him at least a five."

"Didn't I? These glasses are getting so old. It's impossible to see anything sometimes." She opened a cupboard and grabbed one of her paper plates.

The excuse would have been more believable if she didn't make the same mistake every day.

"Besides, a dollar is a respectable tip. You heard him. He was grateful for it, unlike some people."

Darla Jo shook her head and pulled off her cherry-print apron. "Fine. Tip whatever you want. I've got to get to work."

"Work? Where? I thought you were here to help me."

"I am, but I told you yesterday, I'm taking the night shift at Sugar Wave Bakery to help out while one of their bakers is on maternity leave." She grabbed her purse and a jacket from the back of a chair. "A degree in food services is one thing, but I need real-world experience if I'm ever going to have a bakery of my own. Don't worry. I'll be back before you're up in the morning."

Landlady Jenkins scowled. "You're going to be in and out at all hours now? What kind of place do you think this is? And who's going to clean up this mess? I'm not your maid, you know."

Darla Jo looked at the mess and shook her head. "I know. I'm sorry. I swear I'll clean it up as soon as I get back. The kitchen will be spotless by breakfast. I promise."

Before Landlady Jenkins said another word, Darla Jo bolted out the door. I could hear the soft scrape of her ballerina flats on the concrete walkway as she hurried to her car.

From my hiding place, I watched the old woman glare at the countertops and worried she might give in and clean them herself. Thankfully, she only opened her pizza box and piled three slices dripping with strings of mozzarella onto her plate before hobbling toward the living room.

I could hardly believe my luck. The room was mine!

Over the past few weeks, Darla Jo and I had come to an understanding: I was welcome to the batter and crumbs from the bowls, utensils, and pans, but the cupcakes on the cooling rack were off limits unless explicitly offered. It required immense willpower to resist those scrumptious treats, but she always left a generous amount of batter and, I suspected, crumbled a few perfectly good cupcakes to be sure I had plenty of crumbs.

I was especially eager to try this new recipe of hers. Vanilla by the smell of it. She knew I loved vanilla. Since she'd been here, she'd made just about every kind there was: French vanilla, Tahitian vanilla, Madagascar vanilla, and some others I'd never even heard of. They'd all been delicious.

It took only a few licks of the creamy delight clinging to a spoon by the sink to establish this secret recipe was the best one yet. I plowed through the dirty dishes, happily devouring cupcake crumbs and batter and just about anything in my path until I heard Landlady Jenkins talking to Norman Stodges, a video game-obsessed millennial who rented a room upstairs.

When the conversation turned tense, I poked my nose through the swinging door to see what could have peeled him away from his computer. Landlady Jenkins was in her recliner with her pizza on the side table and the television blaring one of her favorite detective shows.

"There is no ghost, Norman. You've lived here for five years. Have you ever seen a ghost?" She popped open a can of diet soda and took a gulp without taking her eyes off the tall, muscular private detective with a bushy mustache and a Hawaiian shirt on her television screen.

Norman, who had a similar mustache but a fleshier jaw and softer middle, stepped between her and the television, wringing a copy of the newspaper like it was a wet towel. "I've heard things, Ms. Jenkins. Strange sounds right above my room."

He opened the newspaper and tried to smooth away the wrinkles. "It says here—"

"I'm aware of what that newspaper says," the woman barked at him. "It's hogwash. All of it. That old busybody across the street probably put them up to it. Well, they'll be singing another tune when I sue for slander and defamation. My great-grandmother, Carson Reginald's very own daughter, turned this place into a respectable boardinghouse, and our family has been running it as such ever since. Do you think it would have stayed in business if there was a ghost lurking about?"

"The article says there have been several reports over the years. Did you know there are laws that require landlords and landladies to disclose that sort of thing?" He reached around to his back pocket, pulled out a folded paper, and opened it. "Our rental agreement includes nothing about known paranormal activity."

"For crying out loud, Norman. There is no paranormal activity in this house. Not now, not ever. Give it a rest already." She waved at him to move aside so she could see her screen.

He wasn't giving up. He pulled back his shoulders and stood his ground. "You shouldn't talk to me that way. It's rude and hurtful. I've been telling you for weeks about those noises, and you haven't done a thing about them. A ghost would explain a lot."

She glared at him. "It's an old building. It's probably mice."

My cheeks burned. I'd been to the attic a few times but not lately. It couldn't be me, and I was the only mouse in the house. There were plenty of spiders, silver fish, and a few other creepy, crawly things, but nothing larger than that as far as I knew.

"If it's mice," he grumbled, "then it's a whole army. Maybe if I stopped paying rent until the matter is resolved, maybe then you'd take me seriously."

A slow, deep growl rolled through her. "Stop acting like a child. You're a thirty-two-year-old man, for Pete's sake. If you think you're going to get out of paying rent, I'd like to call your attention back to that rental agreement, where it explicitly states that renters who fail to pay within five days of the due date will be locked out and their rental deposit forfeited. Would you like me to exercise that provision, Norman?"

Before he could answer, her cell phone chimed. Both of them stared at the thing on the table beside the pizza like it was on fire. When my whiskers twitched, I froze.

She glanced up at him. "Are we done here?"

He huffed and stormed off. As he walked away, he muttered, "You'll be sorry."

My whiskers twitched again.

Landlady Jenkins waited until he was halfway up the stairs before she picked up the phone and tapped the screen. "Hello?"

Her scowl returned. "How did you get this number?"

A pause.

"Well, you have some nerve calling me...."

Another pause.

"You will over my dead body."

She pulled the phone away from her cheek and stabbed the button to end the call before slamming the thing back down on the table.

For a full minute, she stared at that phone. Then

she grabbed the TV remote, settled back in her recliner, and restarted her show.

Usually, I'd crawl up behind the curtain to a spot where I could watch the show too, but all that sugar and butter and flour in my belly was making me drowsy.

I could have retreated to my spot beneath the stairs and fallen asleep in my corner beneath the first step, but I wanted to see Darla Jo as soon as she got home to tell her how delicious her new cupcakes were. Also, I thought she should know Norman was harassing her aunt because those twitches in my whiskers worried me. I didn't know what to make of them yet, but I hoped Darla Jo would.

She never minded when she found me in her room, so I climbed the stairs, careful to stick to shadows in case Norman opened his door. It seemed safe enough. He rarely came down after dark, and after tonight's clash, it seemed even less likely. Landlady Jenkins hadn't gone upstairs since her fall.

Once I was in her room, I breathed easier, and not just because the place smelled like a candy factory with her cotton candy potpourri and scented vanilla bean candle. It smelled like Darla Jo, and that made me happy.

Tonight, since I was already missing her, I pulled

the mini tape recorder she kept on her nightstand into her frilly pink bed under a mint green pillow and pressed the play button.

Darla Jo's soft and dreamy voice came through the speaker: "You are the owner of a successful bakery. You have employees who like and respect you, you have loyal customers who leave wonderful five-star reviews, and your cash register and bank account are overflowing. Your dream already exists somewhere in the continuum of time."

She'd told me she'd read an article once that said the way to achieve your dreams was to record what you wanted and to play it back to yourself every night before going to sleep, so it sank deep into your subconscious. I didn't know if a recorded voice could make dreams come true or not, but when she was away, I pulled it out and listened to it sometimes to feel like she was close.

I must have played that thing a dozen times before I drifted off to sleep, and her gentle voice was still echoing in my brain when my whiskers awakened me. They were twitching up a storm.

This time, I didn't have to wonder what was setting them off because the room was spinning in blue and red lights, and all the noise outside made me forget it was the middle of the night.

When I poked my nose under the curtain, all I could see was the driveway choked with emergency vehicles. I'd never seen so many police cars in one place. And not just cars, but a fire engine and an ambulance that was backing up over the dirt lawn. It stopped near the kitchen door and a guy in a uniform threw open the vehicle's back doors and pushed out a stretcher.

Why did they need a stretcher? Panic set in. Someone was hurt. Was it Darla Jo?

I raced down to the floor, squeezed under the door, and bolted down the stairs, not even caring about the shadows.

All I could think about was Darla Jo. Had she come home early? Had she been attacked? A dozen terrible possibilities raced through my mind.

When I rounded the corner into the kitchen, the stretcher was already inside and it wasn't empty anymore. My heart sank. I'd seen enough crime shows to know what that plastic sheet meant.

Somebody was dead.

TWO

My chest seized, and for the longest moment, my lungs forgot to breathe as I watched the kitchen from my hiding place between the waste bin and the wall. *Please don't let that be Darla Jo under that sheet. Please, please!*

With so many uniformed people milling about, it was impossible to see much of anything beyond the stretcher, but then the crowd parted and I could see out the open door to the street, brightened only by the streetlights' foggy amber glow. A small group had gathered behind a line of yellow caution tape, but one face in particular stood out: Mrs. Dubois, who lived across the street.

I didn't know the woman well, but she was hard

to miss in her leopard-print caftan and a matching scarf wrapped around her neon-orange curls.

Some people called the woman a character or eccentric, but Landlady Jenkins usually used other terms. Ones I preferred not to repeat. Landlady Jenkins blamed Mrs. Dubois for lodging complaints with the city that had already resulted in thousands of dollars in fines. If Landlady Jenkins caught that woman nosing around out there, there would be fireworks, I had no doubt.

But where was the old woman? I searched the sea of feet and ankles and didn't see her familiar orthopedic shoes or polyester pants anywhere.

When two officers who had been huddled in conversation split apart, I spotted Darla Jo, leaning against the counter where her cupcakes still sat on cooling racks. At the sight of her, every ounce of bottled up anxiety floated away, and nothing else mattered. Darla Jo was safe.

She didn't look happy, though, as she grabbed a paper towel from behind a stack of mixing bowls and wiped away smears of black makeup that had pooled beneath her red, puffy eyes.

Seeing Darla Jo in pain like that made my heart ache. As quickly as I could, I found a hole and navigated through the walls until I reached the cabinet behind her. I pushed my way through a worn corner until I was in with the paper plates. I padded to the cabinet door and sat quietly so I could hear what the officer standing beside her was saying.

"Were you related to the deceased?" The officer spoke softly, but I could hear a note of compassion in the question.

"She was my aunt." Darla Jo sniffled. "Great aunt, actually. On my father's side."

I froze as the realization sank in. Landlady Jenkins was the body beneath the plastic?

"And you live here with her?"

"Yes. I've been here about a month."

"I see. Nothing seems to have been stolen and there are no signs of forced entry, so it doesn't appear to be a burglary or robbery gone wrong. I hate to ask this, but did she have any enemies or anyone with a grudge against her?"

"What? No! Why would you suggest such a thing? She fell down the stairs. Someone said she tripped. It must be that cane."

I pushed the cabinet door a tiny bit and saw the officer's jaw muscle twitch.

"How long has she been using a cane?"

"She had knee surgery about six weeks ago.

That's why I'm staying here, to help out while she recovers."

"And that scratch on your cheek. It looks fresh. How did that happen?"

Darla Jo's fingers flew up to the thin red line. "It was an accident, before I left for work."

"One of the forensic people noticed something under your aunt's fingernails that might be makeup. She isn't wearing any, but you are. Did she strike you, Miss Masters?"

"No! She tripped, and I caught her. She scratched me when her hand shot out when she was falling. It's nothing."

"I see." The officer scribbled again in his notebook.

An officer who was interviewing Norman across the room turned her head in our direction and called over. "Officer Caine, may we see you for a moment?"

Officer Caine locked eyes on Darla Jo. "Will you excuse me? But don't move. I'll be back."

Darla Jo scoffed. "Like the Terminator?"

His forehead wrinkled. "The what?"

"Never mind. I'll be right here."

When he walked away, I nudged open the cabinet. "Psst... Darla Jo. Are you all right?"

She whipped around and searched the stacks of dirty dishes. "Max, is that you? Where are you?"

"In the cabinet."

"You smart little thing." She turned forward and leaned back against the counter, tilting her ear slightly in my direction. "Please tell me this isn't really happening. Tell me it's all a bad dream."

"I wish I could. What happened?"

"I don't even know exactly. We had a fight before I went to work, and I felt so terrible about it, I left early to be sure I had time to clean this mess before she woke up. When I came in, I found her by the stairs. She must have fallen. I knew she shouldn't be walking around so much. I told her—"

Her words melted into fresh sobs and sniffles.

"I'm so sorry," I whispered. "Is there anything I can do?"

She rubbed her nose. "I know she could be a little unpleasant sometimes."

A little? The woman was downright mean on a good day.

"But she was family. She was my family. I was supposed to help her and keep something like this from happening. I never should have left her alone. This is all my fault." New tears streamed down her face.

Officer Caine glanced our direction from where he was still talking with his partner and Norman. The way they looked at Darla Jo made my whiskers twitch all over again.

"What's Norman telling them?" I asked.

"Who knows? I can't imagine he saw anything. He never leaves his room."

In all the chaos, I'd forgotten about the argument Landlady Jenkins had with Norman. I filled in Darla Jo as quickly as I could.

Her sobs turned to anger. "He threatened to stop paying rent? I'm not surprised. He cornered me a few days ago to complain about how I was monopolizing the kitchen and that we should reduce his rent because of it. I told him I would be happy to accommodate him any time he wants to be in here. It obviously wasn't the answer he wanted because he stormed off."

"Something else happened after you left. She got a phone call. I don't know what it was about, but the last thing she said before she hung up was 'over my dead body.'"

"Are you sure that's what she said?"

"Absolutely sure."

"That's troubling." She pushed off the counter and paced the floor. When she returned a moment later, she whispered, "Was the call on the landline or her cell phone?"

"The one she carries in her pocket."

"Good. I might be able to find out who called her." She set off toward the hallway, which caused Officer Caine to rush after her. Darla Jo was back before he reached the door.

"Miss Masters," he said, obviously irritated. "We need you to stay put until we've completed our interview."

"I'm looking for my aunt's phone," she said. "She usually leaves it by the land line, but it's not there. Did your people take it?"

The officer glanced over her shoulder to the low bookcase where the telephone sat beside a dusty silk fern. He shook his head. "They wouldn't move anything. This is still an active crime scene."

"Why is it a crime scene? She fell down the stairs. It was obviously an accident."

The officer glanced back at his partner.

"Wait. You don't think it was an accident, do you?" Darla Jo's fingers curled at her sides.

"No, ma'am."

Her eyes narrowed. "You think someone did this to my Aunt Betty on purpose? But why would anyone do that? What evidence do you have?"

The officer backed up. "If you'll just have a seat, we can discuss it in a moment." Before my friend could respond, he spun around and went back to his partner and Norman.

Darla Jo didn't sit down. She came back to the cabinet where I was spying through the crack in the door and once again leaned against the counter. "If they don't have the phone," she whispered, "it must be in Aunt Betty's pocket. We have to get it."

"We do? How?" From what I could see through the window, two men were already lifting the stretcher into the ambulance. I gulped. I hoped she didn't mean what I thought she meant.

"C'mon, I've seen you carry a whole cupcake across the counter. I know you can push a phone out of a pocket."

"Even if I could, what am I going to do with it?"

I'd forgotten to whisper, and Officer Caine shot Darla Jo a hard look. "Did you say something, Miss Masters?"

Darla Jo straightened. "Sorry, I was talking to myself. I do that sometimes when a loved one dies under suspicious circumstances."

The officer glared at her sarcasm but turned back to his conversation.

Darla Jo leaned back again, crossed her arms, and sighed.

"I'm sorry," I muttered, whispering in my quietest voice this time. "I panicked. But do you know what these people will do to me if they catch me rummaging through her pockets, or worse, running away with her phone? They have boots that can squash me flat. They have guns."

"You don't have to take the phone. You just need to find the most recent caller's number. Like this." She pulled her own phone from her purse and poked a green box on the screen then the image of a blue clock. "You can remember numbers, right?"

"Sure. I suppose so." I hadn't tested that particular skill before, but how hard could it be? "How can that help you?"

"I'll call the number and see who answers."

"Like the detectives on TV?"

She almost laughed. "Sure. You can call me Columbo."

"I was thinking of the guy with the mustache and red Ferrari. But there's still a problem. How do you expect me to get from here to out there and back again without being seen?"

The room had been slowly emptying, but there were still a half-dozen people milling about, most of them in uniform, and several more outside. Having one of them aim a gun at me wasn't even the scariest possibility. I flashed on that tiny cage in that scary white room. Worse things happened in places like that. Horrible things. My body went cold and limp. "I can't do it. I'm sorry, but I can't."

Darla Jo sucked in a breath. "I know it's risky." She glanced around then lifted her purse, which was hanging by its strap from a chair nearby. "But what if I put my bag over here?" She set it on top of the kitchen table and pretended to look for something inside.

When she moved back to the cabinet, she rubbed her upper lip and whispered, "If you crawl down my back, you should be able to hop over to the table and hide behind the purse to get to the curtain, which should cover you so you can get to the door without anybody seeing you."

I stared at the purse. I stared at the curtain. I stared at the open door. It could work, but that still wasn't the hardest part. "What happens when I stick my nose out that door? Someone will see me."

"Not if I create a distraction."

"What kind of distraction?"

"Don't worry. I'll make it good. But you'll have to be quick, and you'll have to be brave."

Easy for her to say. Sometimes being brave just means you're too stupid to know you're being foolish. I used to be that foolish, and it nearly got me killed. I'd also lost everyone I ever loved. I promised myself I'd never be that stupid again.

As long as I stayed put and didn't draw attention to myself, life was good. I had a warm spot under the stairs, all the pizza crusts I could eat, and now there were cupcakes and Darla Jo, the best friend I've ever had.

Maybe the only true friend I've ever had.

I didn't want to be quick or brave, but I also wanted to help Darla Jo, if she needed me.

The truth was, I didn't know what to do, and the fact that my whiskers were twitching again only made it worse.

She didn't notice my silence, though. She was watching the window. "It looks like the coroner is heading toward the van, which means they're getting ready to leave. You need to jump now."

Wait, what? I didn't want to jump. I didn't want to do any of this.

"Hurry, Max. Please don't let me down."

The pleading in her voice shot a spike through my heart. How could I refuse? A tiny whisper inside urged me on. *Just do it. She needs you.*

Before I could think twice, I pushed through the cabinet door and jumped onto her strawberry pink sweater.

The impact must have startled her because she froze and gripped the counter's ledge. As I hung onto her sweater, paralyzed, I nearly chickened out. There were still so many people milling around. Any of them might spot me.

"It's safe, Max. You can make it."

She was right. No one was paying any attention to us at all. I had no excuse.

I clenched my eyes shut again and jumped the rest of the way to the counter. When I opened my eyes, the foot or so of space between Darla Jo and the counter's edge made me nervous. But she must have read my mind, because without a word she inched closer to the table, so slowly it hardly looked like she was moving at all.

When she reached the edge, I leaped to the table, where her purse continued to hide me from anyone who might look our way.

"Bravo," she whispered when I landed with hardly a sound.

"Thank you," I whispered back and leaned against the soft, black leather bag to steady my nerves and catch my breath.

When I was ready to go on, I caught her eye and nodded.

She winked and swaggered over to Officer Caine and the other officers clustered around Norman.

"Look," she said, "it's very late, and we've answered all your questions. Do you think we could wrap this up?"

While everyone stared at her, confused by her audacity, I darted to the lacy curtain that brushed the tabletop and ducked behind it.

Through the nearly sheer fabric, I watched Officer Caine look from Norman to Darla Jo and back again. He pointed at Darla Jo. "You heard her arguing with the deceased. Did I get that right?"

"Yes, officer," Norman said.

"You're sure?"

I should have been making my way out the door, but I couldn't believe what I was hearing. I peeked under the curtain to see Norman glaring at Darla Jo.

He nodded at the officer. "I'm absolutely sure."

What did that creep think he was doing? As much as I wanted to race over and sink my teeth into one of his ankles, I didn't have time. I had to get to that stretcher.

I was preparing to climb onto the back of a chair to make my way to the floor when two officers standing on the path to the kitchen door pulled together to block someone who had ducked under the caution tape.

"Hold up, ma'am. This is a crime scene," the huskier one said. "No one's allowed inside."

I retreated back to the curtain to hide.

"A crime scene, huh? Then I'm in the right place. I'm Andrea Vasquez with the Arabella Beach Herald. Is it true someone was killed?"

"We can't speak about an active investigation."

I tiptoed up to peek over the windowsill at the young woman, who wasn't backing down. She pushed her long, blond ponytail back over her shoulder and adjusted her gold-rimmed glasses.

"I see." She grabbed a reporter's notepad from the purse slung over her shoulder. "So, you're refusing to answer my questions? Does that mean you don't think the people of Arabella Beach deserve to know a murder may have been committed in their midst? Or are you trying to cover up the fact that the woman who runs this place was found dead at the bottom of the stairs, just like the man who was killed here in 1903? And if that's the case, are you also investigating whether her death has anything to do with reports of paranormal activity in this building?"

"Paranormal what? No, we didn't say any of

that." The officer sounded flustered. "Hold on. Just hold on."

As he rushed inside, the young woman pushed in behind him before anyone could stop her. She dropped her purse on the table, tightened her grip on her notebook, and marched toward the officers still gathered around Norman.

The husky one tried to block her. "Miss, I didn't say you could enter. You need to wait outside."

She glared at him. "I told you I'm a reporter. May I get your name and badge number?"

Before he could stammer out a reply, a guy from the coroner's office slipped in and whispered in Officer Caine's ear, which made him clench his eyes and rake his fingers through his hair.

When Officer Caine recovered himself, he pointed at the reporter. "You, go wait over there. Someone will answer your questions in a minute." Then he turned and pointed at Darla Jo. "And you need to come with me. You're under arrest."

The officer's words sent icicles through my veins. Why would they arrest Darla Jo? It made no sense. She would never hurt Landlady Jenkins. But Officer Caine grabbed my friend by the arm, turned her around, and fastened a pair of handcuffs on her like she was a common criminal.

Every ounce of me wanted to scream at him to leave her alone, that he was making a huge mistake. But I couldn't move. I sat, frozen with fear behind the stupid curtain.

What good would it do to intervene? I'm too small to help her, too weak to do anything.

But even as the excuses churned through me, I knew that's all they were: excuses.

Waves of guilt washed over me. How could I worry about myself when they were arresting Darla Jo? I tried to think of something, anything I could do to stop it. Bite an ankle, maybe two? Oh, who was I kidding? There wasn't a single thing I could do that would change anything.

"Can I at least get my purse? It's right there on the table." Darla Jo's voice trembled as the second cuff closed around her wrist. That was fear in her voice, stone cold fear. Panic surged through me all over again.

Then a lightning bolt of an idea struck me. Maybe there was something I could do. But I would have to be brave, and I would have to act fast because Officer Caine was already guiding Darla Jo to the door.

With all the courage and strength I could muster, I clenched my eyes shut and ran as fast as I could to

Darla Jo's purse, scaled the side, and tumbled inside head over tail. At the bottom, I hunched down between the smooth side of a wallet and the prickly side of a brush. Holding absolutely still, I braced for the purse to be grabbed and swung over her shoulder.

I waited.

And I waited.

Their voices told me they were near the door, but the bag hadn't moved. Then their voices and their footsteps grew fainter until I couldn't hear them at all.

Something was wrong. Above me, all I could see was a sliver of ceiling through the gaping purse, and all I could hear was that bossy reporter rattling off questions.

But where was Darla Jo?

Then the bag was up and swinging over a shoulder.

Finally!

"You've been very helpful, Mr. Stodges. That's N-O-R-M-A-N and S-T-O-D-G-E-S, right? I want to be sure to get the spelling right for the story."

The reporter sounded close. Too close.

My heart sank when the reason dawned on me: I had jumped into the wrong purse.

THREE

As the reporter hauled me out of the house, my heart raced and blood thrummed in my ears. I've heard humans sometimes faint at the sight of a mouse, but honestly, if that girl spotted me now, I would be the one to faint. It was all I could do to force myself to breathe.

By the time she tossed me and her purse into her car, I'd pulled myself together enough to realize how stupid I was.

How could I have mistaken this purse for Darla Jo's? The hairs on the brush didn't smell like my friend. The wallet didn't either. Nothing at all carried that sweet vanilla scent that followed her everywhere.

This purse smelled of peppermint lozenges and

cheap hand sanitizer, and all I wanted to do was escape. Before I could scramble out, the engine revved and we were moving. She was leaving the Reginald Arms, which meant I was leaving the Reginald Arms, whether I wanted to or not.

Where was she taking me?

How would I find my way back?

How would I ever find Darla Jo?

I closed my eyes and forced myself to breathe. If I didn't stay calm, I'd never figure this out. I had to think. I had to be smart.

Be a brave mouse, that's what I had to do. That's what Darla Jo needed me to be. I had to at least try.

"Hey, Brian," the reporter said. "The police scanner was right. The Reginald story has taken a huge turn. The owner is dead, and the police think it's murder. I just watched the niece get arrested. She's on her way to the police station as we speak."

Was someone else in the car? I stretched up to catch a glimpse and saw her phone in a cradle on her dashboard. She was talking into a nub on the white cord that connected her ear buds to the phone.

"Right," she said after a brief pause. "Of course. But you and I both know the daily editors will swoop in to take this as soon as they catch wind of it. They always take the good stories away from the weekly editions. Remember how they stole my surfing competition protest story last year? And the oil spill at the Bolsa Chica wetlands before that? You can't let them do it to me again. I want this story, Brian. I deserve it. I've already been to the house, I have an interview with one of the residents in the morning, and I'm on my way to the police station now."

We were going to the police station? That was a silver lining. She was taking me directly to Darla Jo.

The reporter didn't sound nearly as happy about it. "You owe me, Brian. I want this story."

There was a longer pause then a few mmm-hms.

"I don't care what agreements you have with the daily side. I've covered nothing but city council meetings, school district elections, bake sales, and business openings for two years. I want a real story."

As I watched her drive, a red flush spread across her cheeks. Her nostrils flared.

"I didn't want to do this," she said, "but if you let them take this story, so help me, I'm going to march into the publisher's office and tell her about your side deals with the businesses we spotlight in Merchant Corner." She scoffed at whatever he said next. "Really? You think they'll deny giving you all those complimentary dinners and gift cards? Fine, then take your chances. ... Of course, I'm serious."

Brian must have hung up on her because she gritted out an expletive that made me wince.

She took a few deep breaths and called another number.

"Hey, it's me. I took your advice. I'm done waiting around for a lucky break. You were right: If I'm going to get anywhere in this business, I have to make my own luck, and if things go the way I think they will, I'm finally going to have a story that will get me off that weekly paper and into a real newsroom. Call me when you get this message. Okay, sweetie?"

Sweetie? Miss Ruthless Reporter had a sweetheart? I was still trying to wrap my mind around that when the car swerved into a driveway and parked. I waited until she had gotten out, pulled the purse's strap up to her shoulder, and was crossing the parking lot before I ventured a peek.

Even if she hadn't said the police station was our destination, I would have known it the minute I saw it. It was one of Main Street's most recognizable buildings, located a few blocks from the pier and marking the beginning of merchant row. This was the busiest part of town, especially during the summer months when kids were out of school and tourists flocked to the local beaches.

The building was a slightly smaller and less ornate version of the twin Spanish-style buildings that stood at the corner of Main Street and Pacific Coast Highway, across from the pier that had been my first home. I hadn't been down here in ages, and the sight of it brought back memories.

My siblings and I had spent many happy days along the boardwalk, playing in the sand, nesting in the sewer lines, and scavenging for food behind the nearby restaurants. Our whole mouse family could live like kings and queens on the half-eaten burgers, forgotten fries, and tossed-aside chicken bits that filled the trash down here, but I was always partial to the sweet treats that wound up in the bins behind Sugar Wave bakery. Sticky cinnamon buns, iced Danishes, and all those cupcakes.

Those old days felt like a lifetime ago. After all that had happened—and everything I'd lost—I knew it was better to put those memories behind me.

I was on my own now, and I had to look out for myself.

It wasn't ideal, but things could be worse. I'd found food and shelter at the Reginald Arms. I was safe there and comfortable.

And I'd done it on my own, without any help from my siblings. Without help from anybody.

Did I really need to chase after a girl, even if she baked such heavenly cupcakes? That little voice inside me whispered, *Go back to The Reginald. You were lucky last time. If you land in trouble again, who knows if you'll be able to escape?*

A cold shot of fear ran through me, and I nearly turned back. I knew the way back to the Reginald Arms. I could get there on my own and hide in my safe little nook.

But Darla Jo was somewhere in that building, locked up in a cage. She was probably frightened, like I had been.

That's when I knew I couldn't abandon her.

Maybe I was small and weak, but I'd freed myself from that cage. Maybe I could free her too.

I had to at least try.

When the reporter pushed through the station's main doors and announced herself to the uniformed man behind the reception desk, I climbed up onto her wallet and glimpsed a long counter with a glass window running along its length.

"Couldn't you have waited till morning?"

I recognized the voice of the officer who had spoken to her at the house.

"Nice to see you too, Officer Caine," she shot

back. "I go where the news is, night or day. Have you booked the niece yet?"

"Andrea, you know I can't tell you anything about that." He glanced back at the empty cubicles behind him.

She twirled a lock of her blond hair around her finger. "Hey, do you have vending machines back there? I'm dying for some caffeine."

He rubbed a patch of stubble on his chin. "You know where the vending machines are, but if you're interested in some coffee, you're in luck. Somebody just brewed a fresh pot in the break room. Take a seat, and I'll grab you a cup."

"Thanks, Mark. I mean, Officer Caine. You're a lifesaver." She didn't exactly bat her eyelashes at him, but she may as well have.

She waited for him to disappear down the back hall then pushed through the short swinging door that led behind the reception desk and followed him into a side room with a long bank of gray cabinets and an old refrigerator.

When he turned around and saw her, he glanced at the window that looked back onto the room of cubicles. "You know you aren't supposed to be in here. I'll catch it if anyone sees you."

"You've always been such a worrywart.

Remember when you were so concerned that Mr. Hicks would catch us sneaking off behind the football bleachers?"

"That was a long time ago, Andrea."

"I know. But it was fun, wasn't it?"

"Maybe." The way he said it sounded a lot more like a yes. "But you're going to get me in trouble. We're not supposed to fraternize with the press."

"I'm not trying to get you into trouble. I just really need your help," she whispered. "I thought maybe you could do me a favor. You know, for old time's sake."

Officer Caine picked up the coffee carafe and sniffed it. "It's already burned. It'll take a minute to brew a new pot." He poured the old coffee into the sink and filled the carafe with fresh water.

She moved up beside him. "Mark, just a couple questions. Please."

"When I'm on duty, it's Officer Caine."

"Sorry, Officer Caine. I'm not trying to put you in an awkward position. Maybe if we could discuss it privately."

He took his time pouring the water into the coffee machine's basin and adding a new filter and grounds. "What do you want to know?"

"Have you charged the niece in the Reginald murder yet?"

He half chuckled, half sighed. "How did you even get there so fast? Police scanner?"

"Who's to say I wasn't just driving around and saw the police cars?"

"At eleven at night?"

She leaned back against the counter. If the room wasn't so bright and empty, I would have jumped out of that purse and made a run for it.

"I was looking for a follow-up angle on the Reginald story that ran in today's paper. You saw my story, didn't you?"

He shrugged.

"Well, plenty of other people in town did. My editor says the news racks were empty by noon. That hasn't happened in years."

"Fine, I saw the story. I didn't realize that place has been around so long. It just seemed like part of the neighborhood up there, but it's what, like a hundred years old?"

"A hundred and twenty."

"Can you imagine what it was like back then? Not just the house, but this whole area."

"It was different. My... A friend dug up some old photographs at the historical society. Main Street was basically a dirt road to the beach. When Carson Reginald showed up and built a general store and a small lodging house, people thought he was crazy. Up till then, there were only a few scattered farms. People thought he'd be out of business in a season, but it turned out he knew something they didn't. He knew a railroad company was planning to build a line from Long Beach down to the Mexican border, and it was going to run right through here. A year after he arrived, he had more business than he could handle, and he put his profits into building that house. There was a time it was considered the grandest, most affluent house in this town."

"It's hard to imagine that, considering it's such a dump now. But if business was so good and he was making so much money, why did his son kill him?"

"I don't know. The records were spotty back then. I couldn't find any arrest notices or court documents. I suppose it's anyone's guess why it happened, or for that matter, why history seems to be repeating itself."

"What do you mean, repeating itself?"

"You read the article. You must have noticed the similarities between the two deaths. Both victims were found at the bottom of the staircase. The owner is a descendant of Carson Reginald. Three generations or four, I don't remember exactly, but it can't be a coincidence. Do you think it's possible the ghost had a hand in Betty Jenkins' death?"

"A ghost? Are you kidding?" He laughed at the suggestion. "But now that you mention it, if I was the ghost of that dead guy, maybe I'd be haunting whoever let my beautiful house fall into such disrepair too."

Andrea pushed off the counter. "So, you do think it's possible the ghost killed that old lady?"

"What? No! You're putting words in my mouth. I was just—OK, I see what you're doing. Very funny. You're trying to get me to say something stupid that you can put in your story. That's not fair."

"I'm just trying to get the truth. I don't know if there's a Reginald ghost or not, but people have been saying that house is haunted for years, so who's to say?"

He watched the coffee flow into the pot. "I think you should get back to the waiting area before someone sees you in here. I'll bring out your coffee when it's finished."

I expected her to argue, but she didn't. "Fine. No milk, two sugars, please."

She pulled up her purse and walked out. When she settled into one of the blue plastic bucket chairs lined up in the hallway, she lowered her purse to the floor.

Finally, my opportunity. After a quick, scanning glance, I scrambled out and dashed along the baseboard till I came to a broken panel with a crevice big enough to squeeze through.

Once I was inside the wall, I paused to catch my breath. The worst was over. I just had to figure out how to find Darla Jo.

I perked up my ears and listened hard, hoping for a clue, but I only heard distant human voices, the whir of the air-conditioning ducts, and a soft chittering, which meant there were more of my kind somewhere nearby.

After avoiding other mice for so long, it was second nature to me now. It was the easiest way to hide from my brothers and sisters, and so far, it had worked. But if I wanted to find out where the humans put Darla Jo, I would either have to scour the building on my own, which could take hours, or I could ask the resident mice. They always knew where the humans were, because that's where the food tended to be.

I only hoped they'd be willing to help a mouse in need, and that they didn't know a thing about the family of talking mice born under the pier.

The chittering led me to a trio of brown rodents working on the remains of a stale ham sandwich they must have tugged through an open electrical outlet near the break room. When one of them caught my scent, he alerted the others. In an instant, they lined up, shoulder to shoulder, facing me.

They didn't look happy about the interruption, but it was too late to turn back. In the black shine of their eyes, I could see the only question was not if they would hurt me, but how severe the beating would be.

Breathe. Just breathe.

No matter what, I had to stay calm, because if I didn't, I wouldn't be able to save Darla Jo. I wouldn't even be able to save myself.

FOUR

THE CLOSER THOSE GLARING, FUMING MICE came to me, the faster my mind raced.

"This is our territory, house mouse," the one in the middle sneered in his chittering, mousy way.

I never expected respect from field mice, but these straggly individuals looked particularly unpleasant. The middle one, the leader it seemed, was smaller than the others, and he had a beet red scar that sliced down the right side of his face, across the spot where his eye should have been. A brawler, no doubt. They all were.

There was a time I could hold my own in a fight with brawlers, but those days were behind me, especially after months of easy living at the Reginald Arms, gorging myself on pizza crusts and cupcakes.

These guys probably weren't interested in a reasonable conversation, but it was all I had.

Crouching low, I tried to show them I meant no harm and posed no threat. In my own chittering, mousy way, I said, "Didn't mean to surprise you, fellas. I'm looking for something. Someone, actually."

"Who sent you?" the middle one growled.

"No one sent me. I'm looking for a girl. The police brought her here. Not long ago. An hour, maybe."

"A girl?" The longer, skinnier one on the leader's left twisted up his face. "What's a puny house mouse like you want with a human girl?"

"She's a friend."

Mouse laughter is usually a soft and cheerful sound, but theirs was so shrill I had to cover my ears.

When it finally died down, the leader gave me a withering look. "A friend? Don't you mean you're her pet, little house mouse? Are you lost without your human?"

That jeer snagged on something deep inside of me. I wasn't a pet. I was never a pet. A captive once. A prisoner, but never, ever a pet.

I rose, not caring whether they saw it as a challenge or a sign of disrespect. "I wouldn't expect you to understand, but she's not like most humans. She doesn't screech and squawk at the sight of me. She's sweet and kind, and she bakes cupcakes. Scrumptious cupcakes. Soft as clouds with frosting that melts on your tongue."

The leader stopped advancing and rubbed his chin. "I do like a good cupcake. Have you ever tried the white chocolate raspberry darlings at Sugar Wave? The perfect mix of chocolaty sweet and raspberry tang." He chef kissed the air.

"My friend works at Sugar Wave," I offered eagerly, happy to have found some common ground.

"Is that so?" A gleam sparkled in his eye. "His friend makes cupcakes at Sugar Wave. What do you think of that, boys?"

"I like their cupcakes too," the one on the left said, and his partner on the right nodded rapidly.

The leader plucked something out of his teeth. "A happy coincidence, huh? I guess it's like the big mouse says, it's a small world after all."

"Yeah," I said, eager to keep the conversation on this happier track. "She's building up her resume to start her own bakery one day."

"A bakery friendly to mousekind. Wouldn't that be something? Scrit, Scrat, what do you say we let the house mouse proceed?"

"Do you think that's a good idea?" the taller one

said with an obvious sneer that disappeared the instant he saw his boss's frown. "But you know best, Scram," he hurried to add. "Maybe he'll put in a good word for us."

The one called Scram nudged his mouse pals and chuckled. Then he swaggered toward me. I braced and tried to remain calm.

"You're pretty brave for a little house mouse." He lightly punched my shoulder. "How about you tell Old Scram what you need to find this Miss Cupcake of yours."

When I told him, I was surprised—and relieved —to discover he had a keen understanding of the building's inner workings. He painted a vivid picture of the network of pipes and beams I would need to follow to make it to the section of the building where humans were kept in small rooms behind steel bars. That's where I'd find her, he said. That's where all the humans went when the police brought them in.

"Thank you, sir." I dipped my head with genuine appreciation. "Again, I am sorry for interrupting your meal."

As I backed away, he winked and whispered, "Do me a favor, will you? Let your friend know, if she happens to find herself with a surplus of white chocolate raspberry cupcakes at the Sugar Wave, she could, oh, I don't know, maybe leave them out back behind the trash bin. I"—he glanced at his colleagues—"I mean, *we* would be most appreciative."

Was he really asking for a favor? Or something else? I wasn't sure, but I wasn't going to question him, either. "Yes, I'll definitely let her know. I'm sure she'll be happy to hear you're such a fan. All right, then. I should be going. Happy scavenging!"

Before he could ask for anything else, I climbed up to the closest pipe and raced along the network of connections until I reached the ceiling over the jail cells. After gnawing holes in three ceiling panels to have a peek, I found the small square of a room where they had stashed Darla Jo.

The room was so quiet, the sound of my chewing had already caught her attention. She was gazing up, and I could see circles under her eyes where they hadn't been before, and the scratch on her cheek was still an angry red. But she was smiling, and that gave me hope.

"Max, is that you?" she whispered. "Please say it's you."

Every one of my fears and complaints vanished at the sight of her. "It's me," I whispered back. "Are you all right?"

"You silly little thing, get down here before somebody catches you. Who knows what they'd do?"

I didn't want to admit it, but I worried about that too. Especially the ones carrying guns.

She stood up on her bed and reached her hand over her head so it was close enough for me to hop down. Once I had, I saw she was even worse off than I'd thought. Her usual soft curls were tangled and messy. Her eyes were dull and red from crying.

My heart ached seeing her like this. "What did they do to you?"

She cupped me in her palm and lowered me to the mattress.

"They took my picture and fingerprints. Offered me some horrible coffee. Then they put me in here. Only until Monday. Then they'll take me to the county courthouse to be arraigned."

My detective show training kicked into gear. "You need to get a good lawyer."

She laid down and curled up around me, so we were nearly eyeball to eyeball.

"Oh, silly mouse. I can't afford a lawyer. I'll get a public defender."

I'd seen enough detective shows to know public defenders weren't the best option, but I tried to stay positive by focusing on something else. I took in the austere little room, which consisted of three concrete block walls, the skinny bed, which was more like a metal ledge attached to one of the concrete walls, a stainless-steel toilet, and a wall of metal bars. That was it. "Where's your purse?"

"They took it, along with my shoelaces, my earrings, and everything else. They said I'd get it all back when I make bail, but I doubt I'll be able to afford that, either."

"But you're innocent," I pleaded. "How can they do this when you haven't done anything wrong? Innocent until proved guilty, isn't that how it goes?"

"That's how it's supposed to go, but there were no signs of a break-in and nothing seemed to be stolen, so they've ruled out robbery. Norman was in the house, but the cops say the scratch on my face and the residue they found under Aunt Betty's fingernail make me the prime suspect."

The worry in her voice knotted me up inside. She was trying to sound casual, but I knew she was worried. There was only one thing I could think of to cheer her up.

"Your new cupcake recipe is the best one yet. I ate so much of the batter and crumblies you left, I thought I might burst. I was trying to figure out what you added. Was it white chocolate?"

A hint of a smile appeared on her face. "Nope. Guess again."

"Pure vanilla bean?"

She shook her head. "One more try."

I'd been sure it was one of the two. What else could it be? "Pudding?"

She made a sound like a game show buzzer and laughed. "And that would be another no."

"You won't tell me?"

She rolled onto her back and stared at the ceiling. "Maybe, if you tell me your secret first."

"What secret? I don't have any secrets."

"Really? Then why haven't you ever told me why you can talk?"

"You never asked."

It was a weak excuse, but the truth was, I was glad she'd never asked. I didn't like being reminded that I was different. That I was a freak of nature.

"Have you always been this way?" She glanced down at me, waiting for an answer.

Might as well make it quick and get it over with. "As long as I can remember."

"How did it happen?"

"I don't know exactly. It happened to my siblings too, but none of us knows how or why, only that it might have had something to do with the way our mother gave birth to us."

"Why do you say that?"

"My mother told us it was an awful, windy night. One of those warm, unsettling nights when the Santa Ana winds howl through the streets, knocking over fences and trees. Because she was pregnant, she couldn't move quickly, so she holed up under the pier, where she thought she'd be safe. Unfortunately, those nasty Santa Ana winds snapped a light pole on the pier above her nest. It crashed down and one of the live wires struck her tail. The electric shock knocked her out, and when she woke up, she had six baby mice to care for. We seemed normal enough, but as we got older, it became obvious something had happened. As we learned to communicate, it wasn't just mouse language we picked up, but human language as well."

"All your siblings can talk?"

"They can."

"What happened to them?"

That was the question I was dreading the most, and it took a long moment for the knot in my throat to untangle. "I don't know. I went away for a while, and when I came back, they were gone. That's when I went to live at the Reginald Arms."

It wasn't exactly the truth, but it was close enough.

She must have heard the pain in my voice or seen it on my face, because she didn't ask any more questions. She ran her finger over the top of my head instead.

"French vanilla ice cream," she said after a long, quiet moment.

"What?"

"That's my secret. The secret ingredient that makes the vanilla cupcakes taste so good. I let French vanilla ice cream melt and use that in the recipe."

"Melted ice cream. I never would have guessed. It's brilliant."

"Not as brilliant as you, Maxwell Mouse." She kissed the tip of her finger and touched it to the top of my head. "I'm glad you found me. I wouldn't want to be in jail with anyone else."

"I wish we didn't have to be in jail at all."

She giggled. "Yes, that would be better. But you have to tell me, what happened after I left?"

I told her about the reporter. "She asked a lot of questions, but I don't think the police told her much. Norman spoke to her, though. When she decided to make her way here, I jumped into her purse and came with her."

Her eyes widened. "She didn't see you?"

Maybe I should have told her I'd been trying to jump into her purse and got it wrong, but I couldn't bring myself to do it. "She was a little preoccupied. Maybe more than a little. Maybe obsessed."

Darla Jo sat up. "What do you mean 'obsessed'?"

"Maybe 'desperate' is a better word. In the car, she called her boss, at least I think it was her boss, and then she called her boyfriend, and both times she mentioned how important this story is to her. She thinks it might help her get a better job. I guess that's what bothers me about her. In my experience, desperate creatures are dangerous creatures."

Darla Jo bit her lower lip. "She's planning to publish another story? I suppose I should have expected that. Do you know when it's going to run?"

"Soon, I think. She's afraid another newspaper will print it first."

"So, this is all a career move for her. Great." She rubbed her bottom lip as her brain gears worked. "What did she say to her boyfriend?"

"Not a lot. Mostly bragging that her plan was working."

"What plan?"

"I don't know."

"And she talked to Norman? That's troubling.

He's been nothing but trouble since Aunt Betty raised his rent last month."

I had a terrible thought I couldn't shake. "Do you think he might have had something to do with Aunt Betty's death?"

She wrinkled her nose. "He's a jerk and a cheapskate, but I don't think he would kill someone."

"He was in the house."

"But he rarely comes out of his room."

"I know, but the police don't know that. Shouldn't they consider him a suspect too?"

"Probably." She touched the scab on her cheek. "It's because of this stupid scratch." Sadness shaded her expression, but she hid it quickly behind another smile. "It doesn't matter. You know I'm innocent, and I know I'm innocent. The police will figure it out too."

Her confidence worried me. She didn't believe she could be convicted of a crime she didn't commit. I, on the other hand, had learned the hard way that life wasn't always fair. Bad things happened to good people—and creatures—all the time.

"How will they figure it out when they aren't even looking for another suspect?"

She sat quiet for so long, I thought I might have gone too far.

I brushed my cheek against her thumb and glanced up at her.

Finally, she said, "I don't think chasing after Norman is going to help."

Her finger brushed the top of my head, and I leaned into it, comforted by the caress. "Do you have another suggestion?"

She scooped me up in her palm and lifted me, so we were face to face again. "As a matter of fact, I do, but I'll need help. Max, will you help me?"

Of course, I would. I'd do anything to get us back to our life at the Reginald Arms. Me, Darla Jo, and her delicious cupcakes.

But what could I do? I stared her straight in the eye. "You know, I'm only a mouse, right?"

Darla Jo giggled and set me on her shoulder, where I curled into the dip beside her neck. "You are a mouse who was brave enough to hop into a stranger's purse to come look for me, which means you're surely brave enough to help me find the real killer."

I laughed. "For a second, I thought you said you wanted me to find a killer."

Her chocolaty eyes disappeared into crescents behind her smile. "I did, silly. How hard could it be?"

"I'm not good at things like that. Important things."

"Of course you are. You got here, didn't you?"

"Barely." I could tell her about my close call with Scrit, Scrat, and Scram, but I was still embarrassed about that. "My siblings used to tease me about my common mouse sense, or rather the lack of it. They would say our mother must have run out of it by the time she gave birth to me because I didn't seem to have any."

"That's not a nice thing to say."

I hadn't thought so, either, but after I grabbed that busker's microphone on the pier to belt out my favorite Journey tune, I had to admit they might be right.

That don't-stop-believin' moment of full-throated glory had landed me in the hands of an ambitious lab coat who thought locking me in a cage in a hidden corner of the city's community college science department, hooking me up to electrodes, and filming me day and night for months, was going to unlock some neural mystery he could parlay into his own moment of glory.

When I'd finally escaped and made my way back home, I decided I could never trust my instincts again, and I certainly couldn't trust a human.

But then Darla Jo turned those big, sad eyes on me. "I'm not going to ask you to do anything you don't want to do, and I don't think you even need to do that much."

"Really?" My fear ebbed a little.

"I've been thinking about that argument with Aunt Betty."

With everything that had happened, I'd almost forgotten about it. "You can't blame yourself for that." I nudged the top of my head against her knee again. It felt nice to be the one giving comfort for a change.

"I know. But I've been thinking about it and what she said about going to the historical society. Why was she there? It couldn't be a coincidence that she visited and then a newspaper story comes out spilling our family tea."

"What do you think she was doing there?"

"I have no idea. That's what I want to find out."

"But how? You can't do much from here."

Her lips spread into a sly smile that made me want to crawl under her postage stamp of a pillow and hide. "I was hoping you might make a visit and see what you can find out."

Was she kidding? "I don't... I mean, where..." I

covered my cheeks with my hands. "I can't do that. I'm sorry."

Her littlest finger pried my fingers away from my face. "I think you can. You made it all the way down here, you brave little mouse. The historical society is only a block away. What do you say, Maxy? Will you do this one little thing for me?"

We both already knew the answer.

FIVE

Getting out of the police station proved trickier than getting in, but eventually I found a vent that opened to the alley behind the building. From there, it was an easy trek through the parking lot to Main Street to search for the nearest storm drain.

Every mouse in town knows the pipes and channels running beneath the streets are the safest way to travel, even when it's late and people and cars are scarce, because cats and other predators avoid them at all costs. So, I ran as fast as I could toward the street to find the closest entry into that underground world.

I kept that pace for a minute, maybe two, before the huffing and puffing nearly made me pass out. I figured it was fear. I'd been riding an adrenaline wave when I agreed to sneak into the historical society, but it was a lot easier to be brave when Darla Jo looked at me with those big brown eyes of hers.

Now that I was out here in the dark and alone, I didn't feel brave at all. I also had a sneaking suspicion that eating my weight in cupcakes these past few weeks hadn't done me any favors, either.

But I couldn't sit around. If I didn't keep moving, I was going to end up a midnight snack for some feline monster.

Luckily, the next storm drain was only a few yards away. Once I ducked inside, I found a safe ledge to catch my breath.

The tunnels were just as I remembered them. Smelly. Some mice loved the reek of mold, stagnant water, and rancid trash. Not me. It made me miss the sweet scent that followed Darla Jo and her sweet treats, and it kept me moving.

When I finally poked my nose out of a storm drain on the next street over, I was happy for the fresh air and even happier that the historical society was just where I expected it to be.

Nestled between a gas station and an office complex occupied by dentists and physical therapists, the historical society's slate-blue, 1930s Craftsman house was hard to miss. It had been the original home of one of the area's earliest settlers, and it was protected by a tall, black iron fence.

Lucky for me, wrought-iron fences weren't much of a deterrence, and the overgrown, blue hydrangea bush beneath the building's eastern wall offered quick access to a slightly open window.

Once I was inside, I paused on the sill to look around. The room had probably been a front sitting room but now served as office space. A desk and a chair were pushed against one wall, and tall file cabinets and bookcases lined the others. Every shelf was crammed with books, binders, and photo boxes, with even more boxes piled on top. Stacks of papers and photographs, newspaper clippings and forms covered every available surface.

You'd think the place would smell of musty old books and dusty files, but it smelled like... I sniffed the air again to be sure. Yep, it smelled like pepperoni pizza.

It reminded me I hadn't eaten in hours. And if I'd learned anything living at the Reginald Arms with Landlady Jenkins, it was that the smell of pizza inevitably meant pizza was nearby.

I hopped from the windowsill onto the photo-copier that sat beneath it and followed my snout. The ache in my stomach spurred me on, but as I crossed the desk, a file label caught my eye. "Reginald Arms" it read in black, typewritten letters.

It wasn't just one file, either. There were three fat manila folders stacked together. "Part One" was handwritten in heavy black pen across the top one. Beneath it was added "Of Four." Before that, "Three" and "Two" had been scratched out.

Maybe there was something here that would explain Landlady Jenkins' visit. I hopped up on the engraved nameplate at the edge of the desk—apparently Charlie Stuart, assistant historian, owned this desk—and nudged my nose beneath the top folder and pushed until the cover spread open. The first page was a photocopy of the news article from the previous day's Arabella Beach Herald. No surprise, I suppose.

Beneath it was a photocopied article from 1975 with the headline, "Former Lodger Files Suit Over Hauntings at Reginald Arms."

Was there something to the ghost story after all? As I scanned the page, I saw a tenant had been seeking damages for emotional distress, but the owner, a man named Victor Jenkins, claimed it was a ploy to avoid paying past-due rent.

Sounded like Norman all over again.

A paper clip attached other articles documenting the court case, including the dismissal that occurred when the lodger was thrown in jail for public intoxication.

Digging deeper, I found similar stories dating back to 1939. One resident claimed a ghostly presence knocked him to the ground and offered the colorful theory that it was Alexander Reginald still searching for his share of the lost family fortune.

Someone had placed a yellow sticky note on the article, drawn an arrow to the words, and written "Last reference."

Was that a note for the reporter? These documents might be set aside for her to use in her next article. I continued to dig until I reached a red folder and tugged it free. There was no label, but when I opened it, I found a browned and brittle newspaper clipping inside.

It appeared older than the others, and when I read the headline, I could see why:

"Carson Reginald Found Dead, Murder Suspected."

An original account of the man's death. The

author wrote in the flowery language of the time, but basically the details mirrored those of more recent accounts with additional details about the surviving family members. After Carson's death, Alexander committed suicide, either out of guilt for his crime or despair over his unpaid debts. The widow, Gemma Reginald, took her daughter, Beatrice, back to San Francisco, to reunite with family there. The article implied she was turning her back on her husband's fortune, which led the reporter in the final paragraph to openly wonder what had become of it.

Another yellow sticky note was attached bearing a single question: What happened to the fortune?

Eagerly, I scoured the remaining folders, but nothing else mentioned anything about the lost money or whether it had been recovered, only ghostly experiences and the transfer of the home's ownership.

It was all very interesting but still didn't explain Landlady Jenkins' visit, though an article dated October 3, 1975, announced the passing of the Reginald Arms owner, a Mr. Vincent Jenkins, who was the great-grandson of Carson Reginald, and that Vincent's daughter was the heir. I nearly choked when I realized the black-and-white photograph of a fresh-faced young woman in a miniskirt posing in front of the Reginald Arms must have been Land-lady Jenkins.

Just as remarkable, I suppose, was the building itself. The Reginald Arms' paint wasn't peeling and the shutters weren't broken. The lawn and shrubbery were lush and well maintained. Even the sign looked vibrant and newly painted.

For the first time, I could see why Darla Jo was trying so hard to restore the place. It truly had been majestic.

The churning in my stomach was making it difficult to keep my mind off the pizza smell, though. Maybe it would all make more sense after I ate.

I followed the scent to the edge of the desk and saw a Pepperoni Joe's box wedged awkwardly in the trash bin. Bingo! I hopped down the desk drawer handles until I was close to the box. With every ounce of strength I had, I leaped from the handle and caught the bin's edge with my front hands.

As I struggled to pull myself over the edge, the bin teetered. I tried to be quick, but it was already too late. The whole thing tumbled to the floor. Luckily, I jumped out of the way before it squashed me. Still, the fall sent the box and some loose papers sliding across the floor. The only thing I cared about was the pizza box. It had bounced from the bin, popped open, and now revealed six tasty crusts ready for the taking.

I grabbed the biggest of the bunch and tucked in for a snack. I was two bites in when I realized I was sitting on top of Landlady Jenkins.

Not the woman, of course, but her name, written in her own shaky hand on one of the sheets of paper that had spilled from the trash. I scooted back so I could read the whole page. There were details about the Reginald Arms: the address, the year it was built, and previous owners, among other details. At the top of the page were the words "National Register of Historic Place Registration Form."

Was that what she was doing here? Was she trying to have the Reginald Arms recognized as a historical landmark?

But why would she want to keep it a secret from Darla Jo?

Before I could puzzle it out, my whiskers twitched.

I froze. Trouble was close, but where?

Carefully, I rose on my hind legs and searched the room, looking, sniffing, and listening for anything that could be a threat.

Nothing seemed out of the ordinary.

Then, something new penetrated the pepperoni smell. The unmistakable stink of a cat.

The thing was sitting on top of a table on the far side of the room, watching me. Every hair on my body stood on end as I realized an attack was imminent.

Scanning the room, I quickly assessed my options. I ran for the bookcase.

In a heartbeat, that marmalade furball was after me.

Only after I had raced halfway up the closest bookcase did it occur to me that cats were far better climbers than mice. It was too late to make another choice, so I kept going. Darla Jo believed in me. She said I was brave, so that's what I had to be. I had to be brave for her.

I held that thought as I climbed higher, scaling one book spine after another.

Still, the cat was gaining on me. I could smell the tuna on its breath, and I hated tuna almost as much as I hated cats.

That hatred and my fear fueled my escape. Even when my legs trembled with weakness, I didn't stop.

But wait, that wasn't my legs trembling. It was something else. With a quick, downward glance, I saw that orange cat's gutter-green eyes staring at its paw on the top edge of a book's spine as that spine tipped backward.

Cats might be faster, but they were also heavier. Finally, I thought, something was working in my favor.

As I watched, the cat scrambled for a new hold, but it was too late. It fell, twisting and screeching, until it landed with a thud on the floor.

My sense of triumph was short-lived as the cat wailed and raced after me again.

In that instant, my fear became raw determination, and I ascended even faster. When I reached the top of the bookcase, I searched for a hiding place.

The cat wasn't far behind. I had to be quick.

A metal container about the size of a shoebox looked promising. It sat between two stacks of thick, hardcover books, but the lid was too high to lift.

The cat was closing in. I stretched, but I wasn't tall enough. I couldn't make it move.

What was I going to do? What *could* I do?

The cat was so close.

I had to run or...

Maybe I didn't.

The gap between the books and the metal box wasn't much wider than a human thumb. Not spacious, by any means, but I could fit.

I poked my nose in and then my shoulders. Wait. I backed out and tried again, starting with my hindquarters, so at least I could see ahead.

By the time the cat's killer green eyes breached the ledge, my tail was pressed against the wall, and I was hunched into a tiny ball of furry gray panic.

I'd hoped the cat would think I'd jumped to another bookcase and gotten away, but its sense of smell must be as good as mine. It hopped on the books above me and pawed at them until it had pushed them aside enough to see me.

Now I was trapped.

The pawing grew more vicious, but the hole didn't get any larger. After a few more swipes, the cat's frustration gave me hope. Maybe it wouldn't be able to reach me after all.

I wasn't sure, though, until the thing stopped pawing and crouched over the hole, waiting for me to make a move.

We stayed that way for hours. At least it felt like hours.

Would it tire of watching the top of my head? It didn't seem so. Every time it shifted, I hoped it was giving up, but it only stretched and settled back in to wait.

And wait.

At the sound of keys rattling at the door, I realized I'd fallen asleep. The room was brighter, which meant the sun had burned away the early morning clouds. Had I been asleep for an hour? Maybe two? I looked up, hoping the cat would be gone, but that pair of monster green eyes were still staring at me.

A terrible new fear struck me. The person at the door was bound to notice the cat's razor focus. If they came to investigate, those human hands could surely reach me.

My heartbeat thundered in my ears, but I focused on Darla Jo.

I can do this. I can do it for her.

I clung to that hope like it was the last cupcake on earth.

When the person entered, I knew by the footsteps it was a man. I edged closer to the ledge and saw a bushy crown of brown hair flipping in every unruly direction around his ears. Was this Charlie Stuart, assistant historian, in the flesh?

"Who made this mess?" He glanced up.

I pulled back.

"Did you do this, Geezer?"

Geezer? The name fit that humorless tangerine mop to a T.

Before I could even snicker, a rolled-up newspaper came batting around the top of the bookshelf, trying to knock the cat away.

"Go on, cat! Shoo!"

Geezer wailed and reeled back before leaping to another bookcase. The man kept after the animal until he had pushed it into a back room and closed the door.

Was I next?

I waited, but there was only the scrape of the bin being righted and the trash going back into it. Then the desk chair moved.

As I shrank back against the wall and took stock of my new situation, a woman's voice cut through the room.

Was someone else here? No, I recognized the reporter's voice. It was the message she'd left when I was in the car with her. Was this the sweetheart who had helped her with her article?

"Hey, I got your message," he said after dialing her back. "What happened with the Reginald Arms story?"

"You won't believe it." Her voice sounded even more shrill through his cell phone speaker. "That old lady was murdered last night. The police have her niece in custody, but I'm working another angle."

"Oh yeah? You think somebody else did it?"

"Even better. If I play my cards right, this could be big for me. Who would have thought a glorified history puff piece would turn into a full-blown mystery? It has everything: family scandal, murder, even a vengeful ghost. Thanks to all that historical background you gave me—and my own touches, of course—I'll finally have a story that makes those daily editors notice me. They'll be begging me to join their staff, as long as they don't steal the story out from under me."

He chuckled. "Looks like your luck really is changing."

"Forget luck. It's about making the most of your opportunities, and believe me, I'm making the most of this one."

"You're welcome."

"What?"

"For the tip and the background information. And... well, you're welcome."

"Oh, right. Of course. That was a big help. Do you have anything else? I'm working on a follow-up story for the next edition."

I heard him fumbling through some papers. "No, nothing yet. But I'll keep looking."

"Great. Thank you. Hey, have you gotten any

calls from other news outlets? Anyone else sniffing around this story?"

"No, but don't worry. Even if somebody calls, I won't give them any of the good stuff."

I peeked over the ledge and saw him pull out the red folder and open it.

"I knew I could count on you. What's going to happen to the old lady's landmark request now that she's dead? Are you still processing it?"

"No, but not because she died. She'd already pulled it. She was only doing it because she thought landmark status came with funding for maintenance and repairs. When I told her it didn't, she walked out."

"She was in your office? Did she recognize you?"

"Nah. She was too busy looking through the folders at all the old articles and photographs. She wasn't paying any attention to me."

Why would she have recognized him? Had she been there before?

"Just as well, I suppose," the reporter said. "I need to get back to work, but I'm glad you called. You've been incredible, you know?"

"I'm just glad it's working out for you."

"Yeah, me too."

Was that it? No sympathy for the dearly departed? Even if Landlady Jenkins wasn't all that dear to them—or to me, for that matter—she was a living creature whose life had been taken. She deserved some kindness.

"So, what's next?" the historical society guy asked.

"I have an interview with one of the Reginald residents at eleven. He was in the house when it happened."

"Did he see anything?"

"That's what I want to ask him."

"If he was there, why did the police arrest the woman's niece?"

"The cops questioned him, so they must have their reasons. Whatever it is, I hope it holds up in court."

The way she said it made me think she suspected it wouldn't, like she knew something she wasn't willing to divulge. Did she know Darla Jo was innocent? If so, I wanted to know what she knew.

"I have some time to kill," she added. "Want to grab an early lunch with me?"

"My boss will be in any minute, and she'll flip if I'm not here. She found out about my side job, and now she's watching me like a hawk to be sure I don't cut any corners."

"Wasn't she the one who said you'd need a master's degree if you wanted to move up? She must know she's not paying you enough to afford graduate school. They're barely paying you enough to afford a car payment. What does she expect you to do?"

"I don't know. It's frustrating. Since I can't get away for lunch, how about I meet you at the Sugar Wave for a quick coffee? As long as I bring back a box of cupcakes to share, my boss probably won't complain. She loves their cupcakes."

"Me too! Can we meet there in ten?"

The thought of Sugar Wave's cupcakes reminded me of Darla Jo. She probably made the cupcakes that were sitting in the display case right now. I envisioned those glorious double strawberry cupcakes with the two-tone frosting and the decadent fudge chocolate with the salted caramel topping. Or maybe she'd made the white chocolate raspberry, or the new vanilla ice cream specials...

My mouth watered at all the delicious possibilities, but this cavalier attitude toward Landlady Jenkins' death and Darla Jo's guilt was still leaving a bad taste in my mouth. If that reporter suspected my friend was innocent, why wasn't she doing something about it?

A sinking feeling came over me. Maybe there was a reason she wasn't doing anything about it.

Maybe this was all a charade that was playing out exactly as she'd planned.

As the guy gathered his backpack and his keys, a little voice inside me whispered, *She said she'd do anything to get out of her dead-end job, hadn't she?*

Suddenly, this all made a lot more sense.

SIX

I'D NEVER COVERED SO MUCH GROUND IN THE sewer tunnels in my life, and it took much longer than I'd expected. By the time I finally surfaced near the Reginald Arms, I feared I had missed the reporter's interview with Norman.

When I found the building still roped off by yellow caution tape, I realized I had another problem. If no one was allowed in, where had Norman gone?

Feeling defeated, I took refuge in a patch of weeds growing around the mailbox near the curb and considered what to do next. All I wanted to do was climb inside my little home under the stairs and go to sleep. The yellow tape might keep humans out, but it wouldn't stop me from getting inside. It wouldn't even slow me down. Landlady Jenkins had left the latch on the crawlspace door open for months, and from there, I could get to just about any room inside.

But even as I considered my options, I knew I couldn't abandon Darla Jo, even if I didn't know what to do next.

What would that Ferrari-driving TV show detective do? He'd find some clever way to ensnare the culprit. He wouldn't just give up at the first obstacle. He'd be clever, and he'd be brave.

As I sat there, thinking, I saw someone creeping alongside the garage side of the house. Someone with a long, blond ponytail.

Andrea Vasquez had apparently ignored the taped-off perimeter and was peering into the kitchen window. When she came around to the front door, she tried the doorknob. It must have been locked because she rose on the tiptoes of her black leather flats and peered into the fan-shaped window above the peephole.

"Yoo-hoo, young lady, are you looking for someone?"

I spun around to see Mrs. Dubois hailing the reporter from her porch. She wore a zebra-print caftan, with her fiery red hair tucked up in a turquoise turban.

"I'm afraid you won't find anyone there. The authorities still have it tied up with the investigation."

The reporter glanced around, looking embarrassed to be caught on the wrong side of the caution tape. "I thought the police were done. I had an appointment with a resident. Do you know where I might find Norman Stodges?"

My ears perked. If she was still looking for him, I hadn't missed their interview. There was still a chance she could reveal something incriminating that would tie her to the crime.

Mrs. Dubois brightened. "As a matter of fact, I do. He's right inside." She wiggled her finger at the cottage-style bungalow behind her.

Andrea wasted no time ducking beneath the yellow tape to hurry across the street.

When she joined Mrs. Dubois, the older woman frowned. "Wasn't it awful what happened last night? Shocking, really. Well, maybe not entirely shocking. The Reginald Arms has had more than its fair share of troubles over the years, as I'm sure you know. You're the reporter who wrote the article about this place in this Herald, aren't you?"

"That's right," Andrea replied. "Did you say Mr. Stodges is inside? I hope he's all right. He's been through such an awful ordeal. May I speak with him?"

That fake concern turned my stomach. She'd made it clear her only concern was for her own future prospects. But would she kill to get them?

When the women were sufficiently preoccupied, I dashed across the street to a hidden spot beside the porch steps.

"Of course, you can speak with him." I could practically hear the plastered-on smile in Mrs. Dubois' voice. The woman was as sincere as a tin can. "He was in such a state when the police told him he couldn't reenter the building until the investigation was done. He looked so distraught, the poor dear. Imagine being pushed out of your very own home."

"Yes, it must be horrible, and he's already been through so much."

Mrs. Dubois sighed. "I can sympathize more than most. Did you know Carson Reginald stole that house away from my great-great-grandfather? It's no wonder the place is cursed."

The reporter had been craning around the woman, trying to get a glimpse inside, but now she pulled back and stared at Mrs. Dubois. "Cursed? What do you mean by that?"

"It makes sense, don't you think? First a ghost and now, well, just look at the place. It's rotten to the core. I've tried telling... well, what I mean is, it's just such a shame. I believe what the place lacks is a suitable steward, someone who cherishes its history. In fact, you would be doing this town a big favor if you wrote a story on my family's rightful claim to that property. I have reams of documentation proving my ancestor was tricked by Reginald. Perhaps you'd like to take a look?"

"That's an interesting idea. I'll definitely give it some thought."

"You won't regret it. I assure you," Mrs. Dubois said with giddy satisfaction.

"In the meantime," Andrea continued, "I have some questions for Mr. Stodges. May I see him?"

"Oh, yes, of course," Mrs. Dubois said, as though she'd forgotten all about the man. "We were about to have tea. Would you like to join us?"

"That would be lovely."

Good grief, she was laying it on thick. I didn't like Mrs. Dubois, but I almost felt sorry for her, getting duped by this two-faced reporter.

As the two disappeared inside, I scoured the house's perimeter in search of an open window, but a rotted side panel below the kitchen window served just as well. I shimmied through and worked my way back toward the front room, where I could hear them talking.

By the time I found a way into the room, thanks to an electrical outlet with a chipped plastic plate, the reporter was sitting in a plum-colored velvet chair with white lace doilies covering both rolled arms. She was scribbling furiously in her notepad.

Norman sat on a floral chintz sofa on the other side of the coffee table, with one eye on Andrea and the other on the window that looked out over the street and the Reginald Arms.

"Did I hear you correctly, Mr. Stodges? You told the police you thought a ghost had something to do with the owner's death?"

He shifted the sizable mass of his rear end and cleared his throat. "Well, sure. It's a known fact the son pushed his father down the stairs, and that's exactly where the old... I mean, Mrs. Jenkins was found. But that was before the girl was arrested. I heard them arguing, you know. Did I mention that?"

As if a stupid argument made Darla Jo guilty. He was lucky I didn't bite those hairy toes hanging over the tips of his flip-flops like fat sausages. Darla Jo was never anything but sweet, even to him, even when he was a giant pain in the... everything.

"Back to the ghost, for a moment, Mr. Stodges. Did you tell the police you've seen the ghost?"

Was she trying to make him look like a crank, or was she really trying to insinuate that a ghost killed Landlady Jenkins? I wouldn't mind if I thought for one minute it would work, but they would never say a ghost was to blame and let Darla Jo walk free. That was too far-fetched, even for a mouse like me.

"I didn't see anything personally, but I've heard plenty of strange, unnatural things."

"You have? Could you describe them?"

She scribbled as he recounted all the scratching, scraping, and groaning he'd heard from his room.

When he was done, she glanced up. "When you told the officers about all this, what did they say?"

Norman shook his head. "One of them took notes, but I don't think he took me seriously. I even gave him a copy of your article to show him I wasn't crazy."

"Was that Officer Caine, by chance?"

"I think that was his name. Blond guy, baby face."

She grinned. "But you don't think he believed you?"

"No, not until one of those C.S.I. people found Mrs. Jenkins' cane in a hallway upstairs, like it had been thrown there. Then he seemed more interested."

"Why is that, Mr. Stodges?"

The man lifted his fleshy, round chin and puffed out his chest. "Because I told him that's where I usually hear the ghost. At night, like really late."

"Do you hear it every night?"

He shrugged. "More the past week or so. Maybe the spirit is getting restless or something. Hey, do you think any of those ghost hunter shows would come out and do an investigation? I know some of them have psychics who can talk to the ghosts, you know, convince them to leave. You wouldn't know anybody like that, would you?"

"Unfortunately, no. But I'm pretty sure they would need the owner's permission to enter the premises. Wouldn't that pose a problem?" She flipped back a few pages in her notebook. "It looks like the deceased's only living relative is sitting in jail, accused of her murder. I'd expect ownership to be tied up in the court system for a while."

Norman sat back. The twitch of his lip betrayed a restrained grin. "I don't know about that. Have you heard of squatter's rights?"

The reporter flipped to a fresh page in her notebook. "Are you saying you intend to make a claim on the property?"

"From what I've been reading on the internet, I think I have a right, maybe even an obligation to do just that. Who else is going to take care of the place? You'll put that in your story, right? That I'm the last legal resident of the Reginald Arms? You'll make sure to use that word, right? Legal."

I didn't have to be a TV detective to know a motive for murder when I heard one. The reporter was suspicious to be sure, but Norman was looking guiltier by the second.

"Sure, Mr. Stodges," the reporter said. "But I can't guarantee it will be included in the story. Ultimately, that's my editor's decision."

Norman shifted again. Some new argument seemed to be working through him. "I'd appreciate it if you would do what you can, considering the unusual situation."

Something in the room buzzed. Norman pulled his phone from his shirt pocket and scowled at the screen before answering. "Hello?"

After a brief silence, he nodded. "Thank you, officer. I appreciate you letting me know." He hung up.

During his conversation, Mrs. Dubois had

walked into the room with a tray bearing a teapot and teacups, along with a small plate of cookies. "Is everything all right, Norman?"

He slipped his phone back into his pocket. "That was the police. They were letting me know they're done at the house. I can go back home."

Mrs. Dubois set the tray on the coffee table. "You couldn't possibly want to go back to that place, not after everything that's happened. You're welcome to stay here until you can find other arrangements."

"Why would I make other arrangements? I'll have that whole house to myself." He smirked at the prospect.

"You're awfully brave," Mrs. Dubois said as she poured the tea. "I don't think I could do it."

"Why not? What do you mean?"

She cringed. "Well, you won't really be alone, will you? The ghost is still there. Personally, I wouldn't risk it." She glanced at the reporter. "Would you?"

Norman gnawed his lip while he waited for her answer.

The reporter dropped her notebook into her purse and stood up with an eye on the door. "I'm afraid I must be going. My editor is expecting me back at the office. I appreciate your help, though, both of you."

Mrs. Dubois lifted a teacup. "But your tea. And you haven't tried my tea cake cookies. They're my specialty."

When that didn't sway the reporter, the older woman set down the cup and hurried to the door. "You will look into my great-great-grandfather's claim, won't you? If there's any justice in this world, maybe that place will find its way back to its rightful owners. Wouldn't that make for a happy ending to this whole, sad affair?"

"What are you talking about? What rightful owner?" Norman rocked back and forth, trying to get the momentum to lift himself off the sofa.

"Never mind, Norman," Mrs. Dubois said with a wave of her hand. "It doesn't concern you."

While he pressed the matter, the reporter reached for the door. "Thank you, ma'am. I'll be in touch if I have any more questions."

"I'm available too," Norman said as she slipped out and rushed away. When she was out of view, he glowered at Mrs. Dubois. "You never told me about any great-great-whatever."

Mrs. Dubois touched her chest in fake surprise.

"I'm sorry. I didn't realize I had to apprise you of every detail of my life."

I tried to follow their argument, but my mind was reeling. I didn't know what to think anymore. Did Norman kill Landlady Jenkins? Did the reporter? At this point, even Mrs. Dubois wasn't above suspicion.

While part of me wanted to stay to hear if either offered any hint of a confession, a bigger part knew I had to get back to Darla Jo to tell her what I'd learned.

Carefully and quietly, I slipped out of Mrs. Dubois' house the same way I'd entered. When I was back in the yard, I saw the reporter's blue hatchback still parked on the street. She was sitting in the driver's seat with her phone to her ear.

The promise of a quick ride back to Darla Jo was more than I could resist. I ran as fast as I could across Mrs. Dubois' lawn and across the street. Once I reached the car, I crawled up into the rear wheel well and found a ledge beneath the bumper, where I settled in and wondered how in the world I was going to explain any of this to Darla Jo.

SEVEN

I DIDN'T MOVE FROM MY HIDING SPOT IN THE car's wheel well until the reporter had parked and walked away from the vehicle. Only then did I hop down to the asphalt to see where we were.

It wasn't the police station, unfortunately, but the Arabella Beach Herald's logo on a plate-glass window told me we were close. The newspaper's office was around the corner from the station, and if I was quick, I could get there in a few minutes.

After my run-in with Scrit, Scrat, and Scram, I kept my nose down as I maneuvered through the building. When I shoved my head through the hole I'd gnawed away above Darla Jo's cell, she was lying on her skinny bed, staring at the ceiling. She spotted me instantly.

"Max!" she exclaimed in a hoarse whisper. "Where have you been? I've been worried sick."

My cheeks burned. No one had fretted over me in a long time. I'd forgotten how nice it felt.

She stood up on the mattress and lifted her hand to give me a perch.

"Where are the guards?" I whispered.

"I've only seen one today, and I think he's taking a break. It seems pretty slow around here. Is that blood on your ear?"

I touched it and winced. A memento from my feline tormentor. I didn't want Darla Jo fussing over me, though. "It's nothing, but what about you? Are they treating you all right?"

"I can't complain, considering they think I'm a killer. A sergeant came by earlier to tell me I'd be taken to the courthouse in the morning to be arraigned. If I can't make bail, which I can't, they'll transfer me to the county jail to await trial."

"How far away is the county jail?"

"I'm not sure. Maybe fifteen miles or so?"

Fifteen miles might as well be a thousand for a mouse. It would take me days to travel that far. Still, I kept my chin up. I didn't want Darla Jo to see me upset. Anyway, it didn't matter how far the county jail was or how difficult it would be to get there. I would go anywhere and do anything to be with Darla Jo.

Her voice lowered. "I thought you were going to be back hours ago. I was afraid something had happened to you. I've been hating myself for sending you off like that. And now look, you've been hurt. I shouldn't have done it."

"I'm all right." I was, but it certainly felt better to be safe and warm in her palm. "I didn't mean to scare you. After the historical society, I went to see Norman. I thought I was onto something. I thought I knew who the killer was, but now I'm more confused than ever."

"Why? What happened?"

Over the next few minutes, I explained what I'd heard between the reporter and the guy at the historical society, and how she sounded so guilty that I raced up to the Reginald Arms to eavesdrop on her interview with Norman, hoping she might reveal something incriminating.

"Did she?"

"Unfortunately, no."

"Oh." Darla Jo sat back on the mattress with her back to the concrete block wall.

"I still think she might have done it, though," I

added. "She's desperate for a big story. She thinks it'll help her get a job at a better newspaper."

"Is she desperate enough to kill someone?"

"Maybe."

"The second she barged into the kitchen, I knew she was trouble."

"She is, absolutely." But that word 'trouble,' struck me. My whiskers always went haywire when trouble was near, and they hadn't done a thing when I was around her. Was I losing my touch?

"What happened when she talked to Norman?"

"He told her about your argument with your aunt and made it sound a lot worse than it was."

"Great. It's not like I can defend myself from in here, but I guess he knows that."

"He also told the reporter he's looking into squatter's rights. He seems to think he can take over the Reginald Arms for himself if it's abandoned."

"Are you serious? Where did he get a ridiculous idea like that?"

"The internet. Where else? Sounds like he's been researching it for quite a while."

"Is that what he said?"

I nodded.

"Well, isn't that interesting? How would he

know he'd be in a situation like this unless he'd orchestrated it?"

I hadn't thought of that. How had I not thought of that? "You're right. That's premediation."

She cut me a side glance. "I think you mean premeditation."

"Right, that's what I meant." I tried to play it off like I knew what I was talking about, and she let it slide.

She pulled her knees to her chest and wrapped her arms around them. "But the big question is, is Norman capable of murder?"

It was a big question, and as much as I didn't like Norman, it was hard to believe we could have been living next to a man who was plotting a murder under our noses. "I wouldn't have thought he could be capable of that, but he seems really eager to get his hands on the place. He was even asking the reporter if she knew any psychics who could get rid of the ghost."

My friend laughed and shook her head. "Did he really?"

"He did, but that was nothing compared to the crazy theory Mrs. Dubois has about the place. That woman told the reporter Carson Reginald swindled the Reginald Arms from her ancestor. She has binders full of documents and letters and photographs that she says back up her claim, and she begged the reporter to do a story about it. That woman is convinced she's the rightful owner."

Darla Jo rolled her eyes. "Aunt Betty told me about Lois Dubois' so-called 'claims.'" She made air quotes with her fingers. "She's been spouting that nonsense for years. Aunt Betty always suspected that woman was behind all the code violation complaints, but there was no way to confirm it. As far as what our ancestors might have done, Aunt Betty had a completely different story about how that woman's great-whatever lost the house. But who knows what really happened all those years ago? Do you think Mrs. Dubois could be crazy enough to kill over it?"

In my book, anyone as obsessed with animal prints as she was couldn't be trusted. "I don't think we can rule it out."

Darla Jo sighed. "What a mess. All these people with motives and opportunity, and I'm the one sitting in jail. Honestly, why would anyone think I'd kill my own aunt over a stupid argument?"

And to think the evidence against her only existed because she had tried to help Landlady Jenkins, not hurt her. It was wildly unfair. Why couldn't the police see that?

"Don't give up." I nudged up against her thigh and wished there was more I could do. Then I remembered, there was some good news to share. I sat up. "On the bright side, I discovered what your aunt was doing at the historical society. She was trying to get the Reginald Arms listed in the historical registry. I overheard the guy telling the reporter that she believed it would get her some financial help with the place. When he told her that wouldn't happen, she abandoned the idea. So, she was telling you the truth. She probably didn't have anything to do with the article."

Darla Jo smiled down at me. "That is a silver lining, thank you. You're a good friend, Max. Who knew my little mouse-in-the-house was capable of so much?"

I had to look away, so she wouldn't see my bashful grin. "It surprised me too. I wasn't even scared." Well, most of the time, but she didn't need to know that.

"You are amazing, Maxwell Mouse." She kissed the tip of her finger and touched the top of my head.

Beneath my fur, my cheeks burned red hot, but I couldn't let the praise go to my head. I needed to stay focused because we still had a murder to solve. "Do you have any idea which of our suspects is guilty?"

She stood up and paced her tiny box. "Mrs. Dubois has a mean streak, there's no doubt about that. But she's so small and frail. Aunt Betty had the cane and a bad knee, but she's no weakling. I can't see Mrs. Dubois overpowering her, even if she had somehow gotten into the house."

I tried to picture the two women facing off, and I had to agree. Mrs. Dubois was no match for Aunt Betty, even a debilitated Aunt Betty. "What about the reporter?"

"Right, Miss Andrea Vasquez." She gnawed at her lower lip. "Her ambition and desperation make a good motive, I guess. And there's no question she's strong enough to overpower Aunt Betty. But what about opportunity? How would she get into the house, especially in the middle of the night? The police said there were no signs of forced entry."

"There's only one person left."

Darla Jo gave me a meaningful look and nodded.

Together, we said the scoundrel's name: "Norman."

Remembering that greedy gaze of his gave me shivers all over again. "If it was him, a ghost in the house will be the least of his worries."

"Why do you say that?"

Before I could answer, the clanking sound of the

lock unlatching a distant steel door interrupted us. The guard must be back for another check.

"Uh-oh, time to go," Darla Jo said. She jumped up on her bed and lifted me up, so I could reach the opening in the ceiling.

"I'll be back as soon as I can," I whispered down to her. "Wish me luck."

"What are you going to do?" she whispered back.

"Who are you speaking to?" the officer yelled back. I glimpsed his black polished shoes at the bars as I pulled back into the shadows.

I felt guilty about leaving without sharing my plan, but the truth was, I didn't have one. Not really. What I had was the accumulated wisdom of too many hours of television detective shows distilled down to one immutable fact: Even careful killers eventually make a mistake. So that was my plan. I was going to spy on Norman until he slipped up.

NIGHT HAD FALLEN by the time I returned to the Reginald Arms, and the place was dark, except for a single light in Norman's room. As I stood under the streetlights, gazing up at that window, I was convinced he had killed Landlady Jenkins.

I only had to prove it.

But how? I thought back to those moments in the kitchen, when the police were questioning him. I'd been too preoccupied with Darla Jo to pay much attention to him, and that had been a mistake. I must have missed a clue. He might have said something that would undermine his alibi, which, as far as I could tell, was simply that he'd been in his room, oblivious to what was going on downstairs.

Why the police bought that flimsy excuse was beyond me. If he was plotting to get the building for himself, as I suspected, he'd had ample time to devise a better cover story. Which meant he either didn't think he needed one, or it wasn't his original plan. Had something changed to force him to improvise?

Could that be why he took such an instant disliking to Darla Jo? Perhaps she had gotten in his way and complicated his plan. If that was the case, it was no wonder he was doing everything he could to make her look guilty. He had to get her and Land-lady Jenkins out of the way for his plan to succeed.

It made a twisted kind of sense, but it still gave me shivers. He had means, motive, and opportunity, and all that planning and research showed premedi-tation too.

When he discovered Darla Jo would be working

overnight, he knew Landlady Jenkins would be alone with him in the house until morning. All he had to do was lure her upstairs. He might have told her he was hearing the ghostly noises and asked her to come up to hear for herself.

The more I thought about it, the more devious his plan seemed. But I still had to prove it, and how could I do that when all he ever did was sit in that room behind his computer?

Unless the computer was the key.

If he was researching squatter's rights and inheritance laws, he had to be doing it on his computer. If the police could see his search history, maybe they could open an investigation? It might not be enough to free Darla Jo, but at least it was a start.

That computer was the answer, I was sure of it. I just had to get access to it. Getting into his room would be easy, but getting him away from the screen could prove tricky.

I'd have to wait until he went to bed, whenever that was. He was a night owl, but everybody had to sleep eventually. I'd just have to be patient.

When I reached his room, I squeezed under the door and found him as I'd expected, sitting at his computer, typing furiously. By the looks of it, he was having a back-and-forth conversation with someone in a chat room. As words scrolled across his screen, he grimaced, crumpled a skinny blue and silver can, and tossed it in the waste bin at the end of his desk. He grabbed a new can from a mini fridge at the other end, popped the top, and guzzled the contents before typing a furious response.

It looked like he intended to be there a while, so I stalked the perimeter of his room to search for clues.

I kept to the shadows to stay out of sight, but all I found were small piles of puffy, neon orange chips, a few loose pennies, and crumbles of a chocolate chip cookie that were too covered in dust and lint to be appetizing. What a waste.

He was still typing and guzzling energy drinks when I'd completed my way around the room, so I found a warm spot beneath an upholstered chair and waited.

As I watched him, I thought about Darla Jo locked in that horrible concrete room and wondered how much worse the county jail might be. Would she have to share the cell with a bully? Or worse?

Then new worries set in. What if I found nothing incriminating on his computer? What if I found nothing at all to link him to the murder?

I was close to hyperventilating when I noticed Norman's screen change. He wasn't in a chat room anymore. He was on a website called Paranormal P.I.s and Spectral Investigations, scrolling through the list of services before moving on to client testimonials. He pulled out his phone and called a number from the screen.

"I'm reading about the free consultations you offer on your website, and I'd like to schedule one," he said. "I live in the Reginald Arms near downtown Arabella Beach. You might have read about our ghost problem in this week's Arabella Herald, and I'd appreciate a call back at your earliest convenience."

As he hung up, the window rattled from a gust outside. He nearly jumped out of his chair.

"Just the wind," he muttered. "Not a ghost. Just the wind."

The man looked terrified. Did he honestly think the ghost was after him?

Wait a minute. He thought the ghost was after him.

In a flash, that little notion grew into a big, beautiful new idea.

While he scoured the internet for ghost hunters, I ran out of his room and over to Darla Jo's. It took all my strength, but using my jaws and nimble hands, I dragged what I needed out of her room and got it in place before I moved on to the next part of my plan, which involved scaling the grandfather clock that stood beside a shuttered window on the upper landing by the staircase. Carefully, I unhooked the shutters and pushed the window open just enough that the wind sent the shutters bouncing back and forth against the wall. I scurried back down to the shadows and waited.

When it was clear the bang of the shutters against the wall wasn't getting Norman's attention, I took a deep breath and let out a low, eerie howl.

Finally, I heard his chair roll across the floor. A shadow broke the bar of light at the bottom of his door. He had to be standing on the other side, listening.

I let out another loud and spooky "Oooooooo."

His doorknob turned, and the door cracked open, sending a thin shaft of light into the dark corridor.

"Is someone out there?" His voice trembled.

"Norrrrrr-maaaan."

Terror flashed across his face, and I knew I had him right where I wanted him. "I know what you did, Norrrrr-maaan."

His mouth gaped open, and even in that scant light, I could see panic glistening in his eyes.

Another gust made the shutters clatter. The moonlight and shadows danced across the wall.

He gasped. "Who's doing that? This isn't funny."

Fear radiated off of him as he stepped into the hallway and closer to the shuddering shutters, searching for an intruder.

Quickly, I hopped down to the first step where I'd stashed Darla Jo's tape recorder and pressed the play and record buttons. Once the tape was running, I lifted my muzzle and called out, "You are guilty, Norrr-maaaaaan. Guilty!"

I knew my plan could only work if the man had a conscience, but I hoped he would confess something that would prove his guilt. When he did, I'd have it on tape.

He was still inching through the darkness, still searching the shadows.

Crouching low, I tried again. "The guilty must pay, Norrrrr-maaaaan. The guilty will pay."

When he stepped into the slant of moonlight coming from the unshuttered window, his eyes were wide with fear. "Yes! I admit it. I'm guilty!" He dropped to his knees and threw his hands over his face before melting into a pile of sobs and whimpers. "I've been filing complaints with the city about this place for months. I had to. That woman was running it into the ground."

Well, that was a confession, but not the one I was expecting. "Wh—"

I cringed. I'd forgotten to use my ghostly voice. I started again. "Why, Norrrr-maaaaan?"

Was that a question a ghost would ask? I didn't know, but my plan was already unraveling. I had to do something.

Norman was still crouched on the floor with his hands over his head, protecting himself from the ghost he believed me to be.

"She was already losing the place, so why let her ruin it completely? I had plans for it. I was going to fix it up long before Miss Goody Two Shoes showed up. At least she did me the favor of killing her aunt and getting them both out of the way."

I bristled at that. "She did not kill her aunt."

My hands slapped over my mouth. Again, I'd forgotten to use the ghost voice. My emotions were getting the better of me. The whole plan was falling apart.

Who was I kidding? The plan had already fallen apart. Norman wasn't the killer. He was a scheming creep, but he wasn't the murderer.

He stood up and pulled back his fleshy, round shoulders. "If she didn't do it, then who did? Was it you? Did you kill the old lady, like you killed your father? That's right, Alexander. I know all about you. I've been researching this place, and I know what you did. Alexander, if anyone's guilty, it's you."

Whatever advantage I had over Norman was gone. He'd somehow found his spine beneath that thick, yellow streak of his.

I might have been proud of him if I wasn't so disappointed at losing my prime suspect for Landlady Jenkin's murder.

What was I going to do now?

I truly didn't know, but as much as I wanted to slink away to my hiding hole beneath the stairs, I knew I had to get back to Darla Jo and tell her I'd failed.

EIGHT

I scrambled down the Reginald Arms' massive staircase and left Norman in the dark. A part of me felt bad about tricking him, but the other part —a much larger part—wasn't sorry at all. He may not have killed Landlady Jenkins, but he was not a good guy, even if he wasn't the bad guy—or woman—I was looking for.

So, I left him up there, begging for mercy from what he thought was his phantom visitor.

When I slipped outside, the moon was high and bright, and the nighttime fog that always rolled in from the ocean gave the streetlights a misty, amber glow. At this hour, the roads were quiet and the houses dark as far as I could see.

But something was moving.

A cat was my first thought. Was this failed misadventure destined to end with me being some nocturnal predator's meal? Not if I could help it. I stood on my hind legs and searched the grounds from the porch ledge, listening and sniffing for danger.

All I heard was that harrowing wind blowing through the tree branches. When I was sure there were no cats around, I leaned into the wind and set for the nearest storm drain. If I wanted to reach Darla Jo before first light, I had to get moving.

I was nearly to the street when I heard that strange sound again.

Then my whiskers twitched, telling me trouble was near. A moment later, I saw a figure. A tall man with the bill of a baseball cap sticking out from beneath the hood of a dark jacket.

He was too thin to be Norman, and besides, I could still hear that louse inside, yelling at his ghost.

The prowler moved around the house, and all I wanted to do was run inside and hide.

A few days ago, that's exactly what I would have done too.

But I wasn't that mouse anymore. I was still so frightened my knees trembled, but I had a purpose now. I had to find a murderer, so Darla Jo would be released.

If I didn't, she was going to jail, maybe for the rest of her life. I'd never be able to live with myself if that happened.

So, it didn't matter that I was sick to my stomach with fear. I wasn't turning back. I would face this danger head on, whatever it was. I didn't have to be a brave mouse, I just had to act like one for Darla Jo's sake. That would have to be enough for now.

I pushed my fear aside and followed the stranger. He was looking for something along the base of the house. He crept along, ducking beneath the low windows until he stopped and dropped to his knees to crawl alongside the dead bougainvillea vines that grew along the wall like craggy tentacles.

When he came to the small door that covered the crawlspace opening, he paused and pulled a crinkled paper from his jacket pocket.

He unfolded it, stared at it, then threw his head back and laughed. "Yes! Of course!" he muttered to himself. He set the paper aside and crawled under the house.

After racing to the door, I peered inside. It was so dark, I couldn't see much, but I could tell he was creeping deeper beneath the building. What was he after? There was nothing down here but spiderwebs and ant hills.

I peered at the paper he'd left behind. "Arabella Beach Historical Society Archives Official Copy" was stamped across the top in red ink. It seemed to be a photocopy of a handwritten letter in florid script. In the moonlight, I could just make out the words:

Dearest Beatrice,

I have not written to beg for your forgiveness, dear sister. We both know I do not deserve it. I can never repay the debt I owe to you and Mother, but I do offer this: Father's treasure is real. He hid it well but revealed its location to me with his dying breath. I have laid eyes on it to confirm the truth of what he said, but I find I cannot bring myself to touch it. My desire for it died with him, as did my desire for anything in this life. I shall be gone by the time this missive reaches you, but please know that when you return from San Francisco, as I hope you will one day soon, your rightful inheritance will be waiting for you in the place you'd least expect, hidden where we once believed all forgotten things were sent.

Forever your loving brother,

Alexander

As I read the words, I knew immediately how important this letter was.

I also had a sneaking suspicion who this mysterious man was: the clerk from the historical society and the reporter's boyfriend.

"Aha! Haha!" His exclamations were unmistakable. I could only imagine what treasure he had found. He was moving something heavy that clanked and scraped like metal.

I ventured into that dank, musty place, listening to his mutterings.

"You cheap old crone, you were sitting on a fortune this whole time, and you didn't even know it. We could have split it, you and me, but you never would have agreed to that, would you? You would have wanted it all for yourself. That's why you ended up at the bottom of those stairs. You did it to yourself."

Had I heard that right? Was that babbling historian confessing to the crime? I had to get this on tape! Where was that recorder when I needed it? If I ran back to get it now, he'd be long gone before I got it down here.

I couldn't let that happen. I had to keep him here or risk him escaping forever with his secret and the lost Reginald fortune.

But how?

Then I saw it, like an answer to my prayer. The door to the crawlspace had a shiny silver bolt lock. As quickly as I could, I pushed the door shut and slid the bolt into place.

The second the door moved, the historian yelled out. "Hey! Who's there? Don't close that!"

He scrambled toward the door. I pulled back, afraid he could break out, afraid the bolt wouldn't hold. But when he threw his weight against the door and made it shudder, the bolt didn't budge.

"Let me out of here!"

Fear and adrenaline shot through me like an electric current. Had I really caught him? The more he banged and screamed, the surer I was that he was secure.

But I wasn't done. I ran like my life depended on it, like Darla Jo's life depended on it, and like every sweet cupcake and vanilla-scented snuggle in the world depended on it. I ran as fast as I could back into the house and up to Norman's room. When I peeked under the door, I saw him sitting on the edge of his bed with his arms folded tightly across his chest and staring at the floor.

"Norrrr-maaaaan," I called in my ghostliest voice.

He straightened. His eyes went wild. He gaped at the door like the ghoul might walk through it.

"Call the police, Norrrr-maaaaan."

"Leave me alone. Just stop and leave me alone!"

He pulled up his pillow and buried his head in it. It was clear he wasn't going to help.

I'd have to do it myself.

I ran back down to the telephone sitting on the table beside the stairs. I pushed the receiver off its cradle and let it fall to the side.

"Is that you Alexander? Are you down there?"

Norman must have heard me because he was at the top landing now. Every instinct told me to run and hide before he saw me. If he did, he might catch me, and I knew, with every nerve and bone in my body, I knew I would never see daylight or freedom again.

Darla Jo's big, sad brown eyes and sweet dimpled cheeks flashed in my mind, and I knew I had to do this despite the risk. Whatever the cost.

The matrix of numbered buttons stared back at me. I pressed the only phone number I knew: 9-1-1.

"Emergency services. How can we help?"

"Alexander? Wait—"

Norman was halfway down the staircase now, peering into the television room.

I ducked under a fern's frond. Could I do this? Was I brave enough?

Yes, I told myself. I was. "Come to the Reginald

Arms," I said in my clearest, most humanly voice, even as Norman stood above me. "The man who murdered Betty Jenkins is locked under the house. He's trying to steal the Reginald fortune."

THE POLICE CAR showed up so fast, I thought someone must have tipped them off. Then Officer Caine stepped out and opened the rear door. I almost fainted when I saw Darla Jo.

She was home, and nothing else mattered. Not the officer, not Norman, not even the historian, who was still banging at that tiny door beneath the house. My friend was home.

As she and Officer Caine approached the front door together, the man fell back to listen to the radio strapped to his shoulder. Suddenly, his smile disappeared. His hand flew to the holstered gun on his hip.

"Move back, Darla Jo," he barked in his cop voice.

She turned, startled and confused. "Why? What—"

"Get back!" he shouted.

Before she could move, two police cars careened around the corner and skidded to a stop in front of the house. The officers jumped out, both with their guns drawn. Two more police cars followed close behind.

Officer Caine waved the arriving officer to the side of the house. Once he spotted the crawlspace door, he gestured at it, and they slowed their approach.

While everyone else's attention focused on that door, I ran as fast as I could across the dirt lawn to Darla Jo. She spied me instantly and casually pointed her toe, giving me an easy way to scramble up her leg. It must have tickled because, as I proceeded up her back, she wiggled and tried to contain a giggle or two. She finally relaxed when I slipped out from under her collar and curled into the hollow beneath her ear.

"How did you get here so fast?" I gasped, still trying to catch my breath.

"What do you mean?" she whispered and tugged a lock of hair over her shoulder to hide me. "The sergeant released me. He said the test results of the skin tissue they found under Aunt Betty's nails matched the blood they scraped off her cane and it wasn't mine. They think it came from someone who pushed her down the stairs. What's happening here?"

"The real killer is under the house. I locked him down there. I think he found the lost Reginald fortune."

"What fortune?"

I had to admit, it still sounded crazy to me too. I filled her in as best I could.

I'd nearly finished when Andrea Vasquez's hatchback pulled up behind the police cars as Officer Caine dragged her boyfriend out of the crawlspace. He slapped on the handcuffs while another officer bagged the letter.

Darla Jo and I watched the reporter rush over to them. "Charlie, what's happening? What are you doing here?"

The assistant historian looked away.

Officer Caine held onto Charlie with one hand and extended the other to stop Andrea from getting any closer. "If you have questions, we'll answer them at the station."

"But that's my boyfriend," she wailed. "Why are you arresting him?"

Officer Caine stared at her. "He's your boyfriend?"

The surprise was obvious, but there was disappointment as well.

"In that case"—he yanked on the handcuffs—"do you want to tell her?"

Charlie stared at his feet, which kept his face covered by his ball cap.

She crossed her arms and jutted a hip. "Tell me what, Charlie?"

Officer Caine smirked. He seemed to enjoy her rage.

When Charlie finally glanced up, it was like a lightning bolt struck me. I knew that face even without the pair of black glasses. The assistant historian was also the guy who delivered Landlady Jenkins' nightly pizzas.

"Those gold bars were just sitting there," Charlie muttered. "The old lady didn't deserve them. She didn't even know about them."

"What gold bars? What family fortune? I didn't see anything in the files you gave me." Her expression changed, like something suddenly made sense. "You didn't give me everything, did you? You used me. Did you...? I mean, it was you, wasn't it?" She closed her eyes and rubbed them hard. "Please tell me you didn't rope me into your scheme."

She was on the verge of tears, but Charlie only sneered.

"It's always about you, isn't it? You complain about your job all day, every day. But you know what? You at least have options. I'm a glorified file clerk at the historical society, and that's all I'll ever be without a master's degree. But who can afford graduate school? I'm working two jobs, and I still can't. I could have taken those gold bars and split without that old lady ever even knowing what she'd lost. That fortune would have paid for everything. But no, she had to come snooping around upstairs when she should have been in bed."

Tears streaked down the reporter's face. "So, you did it. You killed her."

"It wasn't the plan," he shot back. "She must have heard me climbing down from the attic. She attacked me with that stupid cane. I was protecting myself."

"When you pushed her down the stairs?" Andrea shook her head, disgusted.

"Look, I deserve that money. I'm the one who figured out Alexander's cryptic message. I'm the one who spent weeks looking behind paneling and floorboards and all over the attic. I'm the one who figured out it was under the house. No one else did that.

Only me. That's why I deserve it." He gritted his teeth and looked away.

The reporter shook her head. "If you believe that, you're nuts. But you're right about one thing. You do deserve something, but it's not those gold bars."

Officer Caine rubbed his lip, probably to stifle laughter. "If you wouldn't mind making an official statement to that effect, I'd appreciate you dropping by the station later."

She made a show of turning her back on Charlie and addressing the officer. "I will be happy to. It'll have to be a bit later, though. Needless to say, my story has taken an unexpected turn."

"You know where to find us." He cupped Charlie's shoulder and led him toward the police car. "I'll even make sure the coffee is fresh."

"Did he just wink at her?" I whispered to Darla Jo.

"I think so," she whispered back as the reporter approached us.

I tunneled under Darla Jo's collar to stay out of view.

"I'm Andrea Vasquez—"

"I know who you are," Darla Jo snapped back.

The cool reception didn't slow her down. "Good,

then I hope you won't mind answering a few questions."

My friend stopped her with her palm. "First, I have some questions for you."

That seemed to surprise the young woman. "What do you mean?"

Before Darla Jo answered, Norman peeked out the front door and looked around at the police cars and people. When he saw Darla Jo, his lips spread into a wide, fake smile. "Hey, you're back."

Officer Caine shut his car door, leaving Charlie in the back seat, and walked toward Norman. "Were you the one who called about the break-in?"

Norman shook his head, then hiked up a duffel bag that was looped over his shoulder. "No way, dude. That wasn't me."

"Is the caller inside? He just helped us catch a killer. I'd like to shake his hand."

Norman glanced back into the house. "You're not going to believe this, but it was a ghost. I know how that sounds, but I saw it myself. The voice came out of thin air."

"Okay." Officer Caine stretched out the syllables, like he didn't believe a word of it. "So, you're saying a ghost made that call?"

"I know, it blew my mind too. But it's true. This

whole place is crazy. That's why I'm outta here." He adjusted his duffel bag again, grabbed two suitcases at his feet, and headed for his rusty, old sedan, which was parked half a block up the street.

Darla Jo cut across the dead lawn to intercept him. "When are you planning to be back? I'd like to—"

"I'm not coming back," he shot back, sidestepping her without breaking his stride.

She spun around and stared. "What about your room, your things?"

He waved his hand over his head. "Keep it. All of it. I'm not staying another night in that place. It's all yours, lady. The house, the ghost, everything."

The other officers huddling with Officer Caine turned to watch the spectacle. Across the street, I saw Mrs. Dubois' nose on the glass as she watched too.

Norman threw his luggage into his trunk and slid into the driver's seat.

As Darla Jo and I watched him drive away, Officer Caine came up beside her and rubbed his chin. "Is it true? Does this place have a ghost?"

She gave him a hesitant smile. "That's what he says."

The officer nodded but didn't look convinced.

"He's not all there, is he? I mean, up here." He tapped his temple.

"Because he thinks a ghost made a phone call?"

"Sure, let's start there."

I could feel her pulse racing. "All I can tell you is, I've never seen a ghost. Do you believe in that kind of thing, officer?"

He paused like he was considering it, then shook his head. "Is there any chance you know who placed that call?"

She sucked air through her gritted teeth. "Sorry, I really couldn't say."

Technically, it wasn't a lie.

"That's too bad." He sighed. "Whoever it was deserves a medal, or at least a hearty handshake." He ran his fingers through his sandy blond buzz cut. "But this ghost business? They're going to love that down at the station. I may never hear the end of it." He walked away, shaking his head.

He had gone only a few paces when Darla Jo called after him. She jutted her thumb at the front door. "Can I go in?"

He glanced at the forensic team that had arrived to process the crime scene around the crawlspace. When he got a thumbs up, he nodded. "Miss Masters, it's all yours."

NINE

As it turned out, the Reginald Arms really was all hers. An older man in a business suit showed up on the doorstep two days later, identified himself as Betty Jenkins' lawyer, and told Darla Jo she was her aunt's sole heir, which included ownership of the boardinghouse and its property.

When he disclosed the extent of Betty Jenkins' debt, Darla Jo didn't even blink. The gold bars hidden in an old suitcase beneath the house would more than pay off the mortgage and still leave enough for some much-needed improvements. If all went according to plan, Darla Jo hoped to reopen the place as a boutique hotel by the summer tourist season.

On the day she visited the bank to pay off the

loan, Darla Jo baked an extra-large batch of her secret-ingredient cupcakes, although the secret wasn't so secret anymore.

"What's the occasion?" I asked when I woke up from a nap in my nook beneath the stairs.

"I wanted to show you how grateful I am for all you've done for me." She lifted the mixing blades out of a bowl of fresh buttercream frosting and set them in the sink.

"But you already have!" She'd made a certificate of appreciation recognizing my bravery, complete with a shiny gold seal. I never saw that TV detective with the mustache and the Ferrari receive an award like that, so I felt pretty honored. She'd framed it too and hung it on the wall beside the college degree that had finally made it to our mailbox a few days after she returned home. "I didn't even do anything special, not really. The police figured out the DNA wasn't yours. They would have linked it to Charlie eventually."

"Not true! Without your help, they might never have connected it to that creep. He had no prior arrests, so he might have gotten away with it and all that gold without anyone realizing anything. You know, it still makes me twitchy to think he was sneaking into the house after we were asleep and rummaging around."

"How did he even get in? The cops said no one had broken in." It was a question I'd been pondering since the day he'd confessed.

"I wondered the same thing. I asked Officer Caine when I gave my statement at the station." She gently lifted a cupcake from the pan and set it on a plate. "He said the guy admitted to putting tape over the kitchen door latch when he delivered pizza and removing it after he rummaged through the place. He'd been going up to the attic mostly, because that's what he thought the letter was alluding to. He'd been doing it for weeks, apparently, so that probably explains Norman's ghostly sounds."

"I can't believe he nearly got away with it."

She scooped the frosting into a plastic piping bag. "But he didn't because you are the bravest, smartest, most amazing mouse on the planet, and you caught him."

"With a lot of help," I added.

"With a little help," she corrected. "That's why I'm making this whole batch of cupcakes just for you."

I looked at the racks of golden goodness. "They're all for me?"

"All twenty-four extra-special, special-ingredient cupcakes."

I rubbed away the tears filling my eyes.

She grabbed one of the little beauties and planted it in front of me. Then she picked up the piping bag she'd just filled and another that was already filled with pink buttercream. "Vanilla or strawberry?"

Why did she even have to ask? "Both. Of course."

"Of course!" She piped a half-circle of vanilla and completed the circle with strawberry.

I breathed in the warm, sweet fragrance. It was almost too good to eat. Almost.

When I'd swallowed that first massive bite and wiped the frosting off my cheeks, I gazed up at her. "You've been thanking me, but I really need to thank you too."

Her nose wrinkled. "All I did was sit in a jail cell while you did all the work. Why do you have to thank me?"

"I thought I was saving you, but the truth is, you saved me. Without you, I would have sat in this house, gorging on pizza and cupcakes until I burst. I wasn't ever going to trust anyone or love anyone again. I've been so embarrassed about the mistakes

I've made and so afraid to face my family, but I'm not afraid anymore. That's because of you. Tomorrow, I want to go down to the pier and look for my siblings. Even if they're gone, someone must know where they went."

"I'm so glad to hear that, Max. I hope you aren't leaving, though. This place wouldn't be the same without my little mouse-in-the-house."

"Are you kidding? This is my home."

"Not just because of the cupcakes, I hope."

"Absolutely not."

She giggled then kissed her finger and tapped me between the ears. "You know what? You're the best friend a girl could ever want."

When I looked up at her, I saw a world of love and warmth in her eyes. I nuzzled into her palm. "You're my best friend too."

Ready to dive into another Magical Mouse Caper? Other books in the series include *Lessons in Latte by Merrie Destefano* and *Paws on the Pier by M.G. Wetherholt*. Learn more at www.DeAnnaDrake/magical-mouse-capers.

THANK YOU

Dear Reader

Thank you for taking time to read ***Mouse in the House: A Magical Mouse Caper***. If you enjoyed it, please leave a review at your favorite online retailer. Good reviews and positive word of mouth are immensely helpful to an author and always deeply appreciated.

ABOUT THE AUTHOR

DeAnna Drake writes cozy mysteries filled with cute critters, quirky characters, and surprising twists. Under pseudonyms, she also writes award-winning romance, historical fiction, and young-adult fantasy fiction. When she isn't plotting new stories, she enjoys puzzling out the daily Wordle, trying out new recipes, and dreaming of a world without housework. For more information, visit www. DeAnnaDrake.com.

If you'd like to be notified of new releases and have access to exclusive offers and other fun stuff, please join DeAnna Drake's Readers Club: www. DeAnnaDrake.com/newsletter-signup.

If you'd like to send a message, please email her at deanna@deannadrake.com.

Written as D.D. Croix:

THE QUEEN'S FAYTE SERIES

Memory Thief (prequel story)

Dragonfly Maid

Slivering Curse

Shadow Rite

Guardian of the Realm

The Queen's Fayte Box Set (includes *Dragonfly Maid, Slivering Curse, and Shadow Rite*)

Written as DeAnna Cameron:

CALIFORNIA BELLY DANCE ROMANCE SERIES

California Belly Dance Romance Collection Books 1-3

(includes *Shimmy for Me, Dance with Me,* and *Another Dance*)

Shimmy for Me

Dance with Me

Another Dance (short story)

Jingly Bells

THE DANCER CHRONICLES

The Girl on the Midway Stage

The Girl on the Vaudeville Stage

AUTHOR'S NOTE & ACKNOWLEDGMENTS

People often say good things come in small packages, and in the case of a shy, talking mouse named Max, it couldn't be truer.

This charming little guy was a complete surprise for me and a wonderful gift to my writing life that grew out of an invitation from Merrie Destefano, my good friend and one of the most talented authors I know. She said she was developing a light-hearted series about a family of clever, talking mice, and she wanted to know if I was interested in joining the project.

At the time, I was finishing the fourth book in my D.D. Croix young-adult fantasy series and about to begin two new cozy mystery series under this new pen name, DeAnna Drake.

The side of me that is a stickler for schedules (and rules and all things rational and logical) wanted to say, "Thank you so much for thinking of me, but I really won't have time."

The fact that you're here, reading this, tells you that's not what I actually said.

Even as my left brain ticked off reasons why I shouldn't write a story about a talking mouse solving crimes, my right brain could not resist.

I wanted to see what a furry little critter would do when faced with overwhelming obstacles. I was also intrigued by the problems and opportunities a mouse would face if he really could talk and the friends and enemies he might make.

As I got into it, writing about this small creature being forced out of his comfort zone to protect his friend felt really good, maybe because it was at a time when so many problems seem beyond our control in the real world.

After spending so much time in this story world, Max and Darla Jo have come to feel like dear friends to me, and I hope they will become that for you as well.

I'm immensely thankful to Merrie for inviting me on this Magical Mouse Capers journey with her and pushing me out of my own comfort zone.

I'm also in constant awe of M.G. Wetherholt, a.k.a. Gayle Carline. Her wit, humor, and razor-sharp storytelling is as inspiring as it is entertaining, and it's been tremendous fun working together.

Since the biggest challenge for me was adapting to a new genre, I was so fortunate to have a circle of early readers who offered feedback and encouragement along the way. I cannot thank Karen Walker, Janna Weiler, Maria Calufetti, and Beryl Rowe enough for taking the time to help me make Max's story the best it can be.

Finally, my deepest gratitude goes to my family. Their love and support mean the world to me, and they are my happily ever after.

HAVE YOU READ ALL THE BOOKS IN THIS SERIES?

LESSONS IN LATTE
BY MERRIE DESTEFANO

Melvin Mouse can talk and read minds, but he's also a magnet for trouble. So, it's no surprise when he accidentally agrees to help find his sworn enemy—a missing cat. He might not survive this adventure!

Merrie Destefano writes cozy mysteries that contain a dash of danger and a pinch of magic, all wrapped up in a heartwarming happy ending. For more information, visit www.MerrieDestefano.com.

HAVE YOU READ ALL THE BOOKS IN THIS SERIES?

PAWS ON THE PIER

BY M.G. WETHERHOLT

Hazel the mouse may be able to speak English, but she does not chat with humans. Mouse-killers are beneath her. Still, when the property manager turns up dead after a wild party, only Hazel knows who the murderer is—will she finally speak to these horrible creatures and reveal what she saw?

M.G. is a delicate lady of a certain age who delights in knitting, baking, digging for worms in the garden and solving murders. When she's not at home, she's usually galloping a magnificent steed somewhere. For more information, visit www.GayleCarline.com.

HAVE YOU READ ALL THE BOOKS IN THIS SERIES?

MOUSE IN THE HOUSE

BY DEANNA DRAKE

Max Mouse might be a walking, talking wonder, but it'll take every one of his special gifts to catch his landlady's killer.

DeAnna Drake writes cozy mysteries filled with cute critters, quirky characters, and surprising twists. For more information, visit www.DeAnnaDrake.com.